One In A Million

NICHOLAS READ

One In A Million

Copyright © 1996 by Nicholas Read

Second edition published in 2000

No part of this publication may be reproduced, stored in a retrieval system or transmitted in any form or by any means without prior written permission from the publisher, or, in case of photocopying or other reprographic copying, a licence from CANCOPY (Canadian Copyright Licensing Agency), One Yonge Street, Suite 1900, Toronto, Ontario, M5E 1E5.

Polestar Book Publishers and Raincoast Books acknowledge the ongoing support of The Canada Council; the British Columbia Ministry of Small Business, Tourism and Culture through the BC Arts Council; and the Government of Canada through the Book Publishing Industry Development Program (BPIDP).

Interior and cover illustrations by Chum McLeod
Cover design by Ingrid Lund
Editing by Kim Nash

Printed and bound in Canada.

Canadian Cataloguing in Publication Data

Nicholas Read, 1956 –
        One in a million

ISBN 1-896095-22-4

I. Dogs — Jeuvenile fiction. I Title.
PS8585.E22O63 1996   j813'.54   C96-910412-X
PZ7.R22On 1996

Polestar Book Publishers
An imprint of Raincoast Books
9050 Shaughnessy Street
Vancouver, B.C.
V6P 6E5

10 9 8 7 6 5 4 3 2

ONE IN A MILLION

Nicholas Read

POLESTAR

To Karen Adirim, a man's best friend

one

JOEY WAS SCARED. His brothers and sisters were scared too because none of them knew what was happening. All they knew was that one minute they were playing happily and cuddling close to their mother, and the next they were thrown willy-nilly onto a cold, hard desktop, looking up into the face of a stranger.

"What's happening?" said one.

"Where's our mum?" asked another.

But Joey didn't know. None of them did. They couldn't even guess. It was all too new and different.

Then the stranger spoke. "Not more pups!" he shouted, slapping his hand against his forehead. "You were here six months ago with six other dogs. And six months before that. When are you going to learn?"

"Look, if I'm gonna get a lecture every time I come in here, I ain't gonna come in here no more, you hear me?" a second voice replied. This was a voice Joey knew. It belonged to Mr. Hunter, the master of Joey's mother.

"I don't even know why you keep a dog," said the first man, whose name was Mr. McNulty. "You haven't even given her a name. You let her run wild, and every six months she has pups which you bring here. It's not good for a dog. It'll make her old before her time."

"Then I'll get another dog," growled Mr. Hunter through his grizzly beard. "It's my business, not yours. And if you keep bellyachin' at me, the next litter o' pups is goin' in the river. Understand?"

Mr. McNulty just sighed. Some people were worth talking to; some people weren't. Mr. Hunter wasn't. So he gathered together the pups, and decided not to argue with him any more. Mr. McNulty was an official at the local animal shelter, and he knew when it was time to give up.

"They look like shepherd crosses again," he finally said, lifting one of Joey's brothers off the desk top and into a box. "Not much bigger than a football, are they? But they'll grow all right. Too bad because most of the people who come in here want small dogs that'll fit on their laps. Oh well, at least they're pups. Pups always have a better chance than grown dogs."

"Yeah, they're shepherd crosses. Smart dogs. They can pick things up real quick. You can't go wrong with one."

"Is that why you keep breeding them?" Mr. McNulty asked, putting the rest of the pups in the box.

Mr. Hunter didn't reply. He just stared at the man, his squinty grey eyes squinting even harder than usual. He'd had enough. "It's not my business," he growled. "It's yours now. Do what you want with 'em."

Then he turned on his heel and left, not to be seen again until Joey's mother gave birth to yet another litter.

"Where are we?" whimpered one of Joey's sisters as she looked up at the strange man staring down at her from over the rim of the box. "What is this place?"

They all sensed it wasn't a happy place, and they worried they might be in some kind of trouble.

"I don't know, but I wish we weren't here," was all Joey could think to say.

"Me too," said his brother. "I wish we were back with our mum."

Instead, they were taken to the back of the shelter to a cage built specially for puppies. It was the size of a large closet and was made of concrete and wire mesh like a schoolyard fence. Its door was kept locked so that the dogs couldn't get out of the cage and people couldn't get into it. Mr. McNulty unlocked the door and set the box down onto the floor. Then without saying a word, he took the pups out of the box one by one and left them, locking the door behind him as he went.

The cage floor was as hard and cold as a sidewalk. Joey and his brothers and sisters huddled together to keep warm — they felt safer that way too.

"How long do you think we'll have to stay here?" one of Joey's sisters asked, pressing even closer to him. But she didn't get an answer because none of the pups knew.

All they did know was that this had been the worst day of their short lives. Clutched together in one corner of the cage, they looked like an old fur stole that someone had tossed aside. Sometimes the stole would move when one of the pups tried to push his way tighter into the circle or if another was pushed out of it by mistake. But when that happened, room was made again for him quickly. Each pup needed to have the others close by, and that's how they stayed for the rest of the day and all that night.

They were awakened the next morning by the sound of the cage door being opened.

"Here you are, pups," called a cheerful voice as a tray of food was set down. "Eat hearty."

The tray was three times the size of any of them, and they jumped when they heard the harsh, scraping sound it made as it was pushed across the floor. But their hunger overcame their fear, and soon Joey, who was the oldest of the litter by a minute or two, and the bravest, broke away to inspect the tray. His little nose worked like an engine as he sniffed the floor of the cage, then the tray, and finally the food itself. When he realized what it was, he began gobbling it up as if he hadn't eaten for days.

"Come on," he urged the others. "Come and get it. It's good and I'm hungry."

Seeing him safe beside the tray, his brothers and sisters began to make their way toward it, and soon they were all jostling for a spot and digging in.

It was then that they looked more closely at the other pups in the cage. They'd seen them the day before, but were too afraid to approach them. Now, Joey decided, it might be time to say hello. The other pups were all black and had large floppy ears the size and shape of potato chips, unlike Joey's ears which were shaped like triangles and stood upright. The other pups were also thinner than Joey, who was built like a little tractor. But they seemed friendly, and Joey, being a curious fellow, wanted to get to know them.

"Hello," he yipped, sniffing the first black pup he came to. "Who are you?"

"Blackie," said the pup. "This is my brother and sister," he said, turning to the other black pups in the cage. Joey nodded hello to them.

"I saw you come in yesterday," Blackie said. "How did you get here?"

"A man brought us," Joey replied. "He lives in our house. But yesterday he put us in a basket and brought us here."

"So he didn't want you. A lot of pups end up here because people don't want them."

Even though he was no more than three months old, Blackie already knew a lot more about the world than Joey did.

"Why not?" Joey asked, shocked. "Why don't people want them?"

"I don't know," Blackie replied sadly. "But people are

always bringing in pups they don't want. Grown-up dogs too. That's how most of those dogs got here." He looked toward a row of nearby cages where adult dogs were kept. All of them looked as sad as Joey's mother had when Joey was taken away from her. Sometimes one of them would even lift its head and howl exactly the way she had. It was terrible for Joey to hear.

"Is that how you got here?" Joey asked Blackie.

"No, my sister and brother and I were brought in by one of the men who work here. He found us in a garbage can. I don't remember how we got there, but that's where he found us. I had two other brothers, but they died, so the man who brought us here took them away."

"Where to?" asked Joey.

"I don't know," Blackie said. "Just away. So now there are only the three of us left."

"But didn't anyone want you either?" Joey asked, the worry welling in him like water in a barrel.

"I don't remember," Blackie replied. "I don't remember anything before the garbage can." Then he paused and turned his head. "You see that pup over there?" He gestured toward a bedraggled looking brown and white pit bull terrier that was huddled by itself in a corner. "He was thrown out of a moving car. The people who had him just opened the door and threw him out. Then someone else found him and brought him here. I don't think he's hurt, but he never talks to anyone. He told us what happened and then he never said another word."

Joey didn't know what to say. It was all so much to take in. He couldn't understand why someone wouldn't want him and the other dogs. What was wrong with them? Had they all done something bad? Had he?

"So what is this place?" he finally asked Blackie.

"It's a just a place for animals like us," Blackie said. "Animals who have nowhere else to go. We stay here 'til we find homes. If we find homes. Some animals don't."

"They don't?" Joey asked. "Then what happens to them?" He was barely able to squeak out the words.

"I don't know. They're just taken away. But don't worry," he said after a while. He could see how frightened Joey had become. "Griff told me that pups have a much better chance of finding a home than grown-up dogs do. So you'll probably find a home really soon."

"I hope so," said Joey, his voice quavering a little. "But who's Griff? And why don't people want grown-up dogs?" Asking this made Joey think of his mother. He hated to think that someone wouldn't want her.

"Griff was the old dog who told me about the shelter. The shelter people put him in here with us because there was no room for him in the grown-up cages."

"What happened to him?" asked Joey. "Did he find a home?"

"I don't think so," said Blackie. "One day one of the shelter men came by and took him away. And then we never saw him again."

Joey's heart pounded like a drum. Even if it were true

that people wanted pups more than older dogs, what if no one wanted him? He shut his eyes and tried not to think about it. In fact, he tried not to think about anything, but it wasn't easy. Everything Blackie had said sounded bad. So he ran back to where his brothers and sisters were, and buried his face in their fur.

The next day was a little better. Joey tried hard to put Blackie's words out of his mind, and decided to explore the cage. There wasn't much room to explore, even for a pup Joey's size, but what there was, he investigated thoroughly, sniffing every inch of the floor and the wire mesh walls as high as he could reach. He also sniffed the other pups in the cage so he could get to know them, and tried to make friends with the little pit bull who had been thrown out of the car. But Blackie was right, he wouldn't say anything to him.

The other pups were friendlier, and soon they were rolling around with each other, wrestling and growling, and chasing each other's tails. It was great fun. It even got so that Joey forgot where he was for a few minutes. But then one of the pups would start gnawing at the wire door with his pebbly teeth, and Joey would copy him and get cross. He'd remember what Blackie had said, and start to cry. Sometimes it seemed he would never stop crying, but then he would get tired, and just like that, almost in the time it takes to breathe in and out, he'd fall asleep.

It went on like this for days. Joey would wait and worry,

play with the other pups, cry sometimes, and then fall suddenly into a restless sleep.

One day one of the pups was lucky enough to be adopted. Joey yapped as loudly as he could at the people who came in, but even though they picked him up and said nice things to him, they left him behind and took the other pup instead. "I suppose they didn't want me," Joey thought to himself afterwards. "I wonder if anyone will."

But two days later someone did.

A boy dragging his parents around the shelter courtyard picked Joey out from behind the wire door as soon as he saw him. "That's the one I want!" the boy shouted to his mother. "The black one with the brown bits on his ears and tail."

The boy was ten years old, and dressed like an army commando in olive green imitation fatigues and high-top sneakers. His mother was dressed more elegantly with rings on her fingers, high heels and a designer coat, and she was worried about getting dirty. To her and the boy's father, all the dogs looked black with brown bits on their ears and tails.

"Fine, Robert," said his mother as enthusiastically as she could. "Choose the one you want. Just choose it quickly so we can get away from all this barking."

All the shelter dogs, big and small, had started barking, as if to say "Pick me! Pick me!" when they caught sight of the three strangers. The noise was deafening, and though some people who came through the shelter felt sorry for the dogs, others were just annoyed.

"He wants that one," the boy's mother informed the shelter attendant who was sweeping nearby. "The one with the ears and the tail." Then realizing that all the dogs had ears and a tail, she said, embarrassed: "Oh, you know what I mean, that one," pointing at Joey. "Could you please get him for us?"

The attendant unlocked the door, and Joey, who was almost hoarse from barking so much, was lifted into Robert's eager arms. Robert had never had a dog, and Joey had never had a proper master, yet they took to each other instantly. Some puppies are shy; others are bold as soldiers. Joey was a soldier, so he wasted no time being coy. He was all over Robert like a wash, licking his delighted face, burrowing his nose under Robert's arms, and wriggling and squiggling like a worm.

"Isn't he great, Mum?" Robert exclaimed, laughing as Joey scrambled all over him. "Isn't he the greatest dog you've ever seen?"

"Yes, Robert, he's very cute," replied Mrs. LeClerc. "But we're in a hurry so let's take him away as quickly as we can, all right?" Mrs. LeClerc had had enough of the din, and now, studying Joey more closely, was a little alarmed at how excited he was. She and her husband thought it would be good for Robert to have a dog, but at the same time they were a little unsure of what it would mean. Seeing how energetic Joey was, she was more uncertain than ever. Her neighbours, the Booths, had had to get rid of their dog a few weeks ago because of all the noise and mess it had made. The dog had seemed fine when it was a puppy, but then it had grown bigger than anyone expected. So the Booths took it back to the animal shelter. Mrs. Booth had told Mrs. LeClerc that she was sorry to have to do it, but she couldn't cope. The dog was too much trouble.

Now Mrs. LeClerc worried that she was about to make the same mistake. But Robert had promised that he would look after the dog, and Robert was a responsible boy, so maybe ... "Oh well," she thought, collecting herself, "I'll worry about the future when it comes. Besides, I'm sure the dog will be fine. That Mrs. Booth is always making a fuss about nothing."

So while Robert and Joey fell over each other with newly found affection, Mr. and Mrs. LeClerc filled out Joey's adoption papers and assured Mr. McNulty that they would be good to Joey. Yes, they would train him, they promised. Yes, they had a fenced yard so he couldn't run loose. Yes, they would have him neutered when he was six months old so he couldn't father any unwanted pups. It was all done as quickly and efficiently as possible.

But Joey didn't care about any of that. All that mattered was that someone wanted him after all. He was so happy he thought he could fly. He almost did when Robert stumbled and dropped him. The fall gave him quite a start, and he yelped with surprise when he hit the ground. But he wasn't hurt. Nor was he mad at Robert. He already loved Robert too much for that. In fact, he was so excited that he almost forgot to think about the pups he was leaving behind. At the last minute, he called out: "Good-bye, everybody, good-bye." But they couldn't hear him. He was already too far away. Robert just thought he was barking at him.

two

THE LECLERCS LIVED in a big house in a nice part of the city. It had been decorated from top to bottom by an interior designer, and was filled with antique furniture, porcelain china and crystal so delicate that a whisper might shatter it. It was not the sort of house for a lively new puppy, especially a puppy as young as Joey. The LeClercs realized that as soon as they got home. Joey had been excited all the way from the shelter, and he still hadn't calmed down. When they let him in the house, he twisted and turned like a little black top. Robert tried to catch him, but Joey was too fast, and he slipped under the sofa where he peed on the spot.

Mrs. LeClerc's shrieks almost brought the house down. "Get that dog out of here!" she yelled at Robert, who was already down on his hands and knees rescuing Joey. She was not the sort of woman to yell at anyone, but she hadn't expected this — not on her beautiful rug. No, if Robert was going to have a dog, she decided, he was going to have to learn to control it.

"Put him out in the backyard," she said more calmly but still sternly. "Quickly, Robert, before he makes a mess somewhere else."

Robert was surprised at how angry his mother was. Normally, he could handle her pretty easily, but there would be no talking to her this time. This time she was too upset.

"Okay, okay," he said. "Joey didn't mean to do it."

"I don't care what he meant to do," scolded Mrs. LeClerc. "I just want him out of this room before he messes it again."

Joey was stunned by Mrs. LeClerc's outburst. What was she so angry about, he wondered. What had he done wrong? He was still too young to know that he shouldn't go to the bathroom in the house. So he cowered with fright under the sofa and didn't want to come out until all the shouting was over.

Robert pulled him out from his hiding place, and took him to the backyard. Joey, who was relieved to be back in Robert's arms, liked the yard as soon as he saw it. It was big and full of trees, bushes and fascinating smells that he couldn't wait to investigate. So forgetting what had happened in the living room, he began to scoop up the smells like a vacuum cleaner while Robert, who was kneeling nearby, watched him and laughed.

It had taken Robert a while to convince his parents to let him have a dog. Usually, they gave him whatever he wanted, but getting a dog had been different. They said a dog might be too much work and responsibility for him. Responsibility was a word they used over and over again. It meant that looking after the dog would be his job, and no one else's. They worried that he might not be up to it what with his schoolwork, his Saturday soccer and his computer club. But Robert was determined, and in the end they gave in. Now it was up to Robert to show them how wrong they had been to worry. He had to show them that a dog wasn't too much trouble to look after. In fact, he had to show them that it was no trouble at all. If only Joey hadn't peed on the carpet. His mum might take a while to get over that. He waited half an hour or so before he dared go back inside to see if the storm was over.

"Mum?" he called out in a soft, sweet voice as he tiptoed through the kitchen and into the living room. "Mum, are you still mad?"

His mother, who had been down on her knees scrubbing the spot where Joey had had his accident, was just getting up. She looked tired, and a few strands of hair fell loosely over her face. Seeing her that way made Robert worry all over again, but it turned out there was no need. "No, no, everything's fine," she said, straightening her hair. "I've got the dirt out now. But this carpet is very expensive, and I don't want Joey peeing on it again. Do you understand?"

"Yes, I understand. It won't happen again. Joey's out

in the backyard now smelling things. So he won't be any trouble any more. He'll go to the bathroom out there."

"That's good. But what about next time? Are you going to train him to go to the bathroom outside all the time? Remember, Robert, he's your dog, and you're the one who has to look after him."

"I know, I know," Robert said crossly. He hated it when his mum treated him like a kid. He knew how to look after Joey. As long as he fed him and loved him and played with him, Joey would be fine. Everything else, he thought, would take care of itself.

That night, after Joey had spent the whole day outside rooting around the LeClercs' bushes and trees, tumbling on their grass, and falling asleep from time to time in Robert's cradling arms, Robert brought him inside and insisted that he sleep with him on his bed. "He'll be fine," Robert told his parents. Then to Joey: "You want to sleep here, don't you?"

Joey was happy to go along with anything Robert suggested. He loved being the centre of so much attention. Even if Robert's parents did give him the odd disapproving look, Robert was crazy about him. And as soon as Joey was dropped onto Robert's bed, he was crazy about that too. It was so cozy and warm and soft — much better than the hard, dirty floor at the animal shelter.

Robert was excited to have Joey on his bed too, and it

was a long time before either of them settled down. Finally they did sleep, but it was only a few hours before Robert woke up yelling.

"Awww, Joey," he cried. "What did you go and do that for?"

The part of the bed where Joey was sleeping was all wet.

Mr. and Mrs. LeClerc rushed into the bedroom, worried that something dreadful had happened. "Oh, Robert," said his mother, tying up her dressing gown cord. "Now look what's happened. I knew we shouldn't have let Joey sleep with you. Now we'll have to change your sheets, and it's after one o'clock in the morning."

Joey had no idea what the fuss was about. These people were so strange, he thought. First they loved him and put him in a nice, soft bed; then they yelled at him. Had he done something terrible? "Oh no," he thought, "maybe they won't want me now." The thought frightened him so much that he started to whimper, but the LeClercs were too busy stripping Robert's bed to notice.

"Now, Robert," said Mrs. LeClerc as she pulled the wet sheets off the mattress. "You and your father had better find Joey a box to sleep in and put him in the kitchen for the rest of the night, okay?"

By this point, Robert was angry with Joey too, so he didn't mind taking him away. He didn't even mind his mother's scolding. All he wanted was to get back to a dry bed. So while Mrs. LeClerc was left to clean up Joey's mess, Robert and his dad found an empty box for Joey and put him in the kitchen. Robert was ready to leave him like that, but Mr. LeClerc found an old towel to line the box with so Joey would be more comfortable. He also had heard that puppies like sleeping with a ticking clock because the sound reminded them of their mother's heartbeat. But when he went looking for one, he found that all the clocks in the house were digital, so Joey had to do without.

Joey had been upset by Robert's shouting, but this seemed like another game. The box, the towel, the butter yellow kitchen — they were all new to him, and he was eager to have Robert join in his explorations. So he didn't understand when Robert and Mr. LeClerc shut the kitchen door and left him behind on his own.

Bewildered and frightened, he started to whimper again — then howl, making a terrible, piercing noise that filled the house. At first, the LeClercs tried to ignore it, thinking Joey would soon calm down and drift off to sleep. But no sooner did he stop for a few minutes, than he would start up again as loudly as before. It happened again and again. After a while the LeClercs found themselves listening for him to start each time he stopped. Sleep was impossible, and after nearly an hour, they trooped back to the kitchen and moved Joey and his box to the basement where they knew they wouldn't hear him. Robert thought it was a little harsh, but even he was tired of Joey's whining too, and didn't object too much.

Joey continued to whimper and whine in the basement. It reminded him of the animal shelter except it was more shadowy. He was cold despite the towel, and sometimes the furnace would bang suddenly, scaring him and making him cry even louder. But no one heard him, and no one came to see him. Every now and then he would fall asleep because he couldn't keep his eyes open any longer, but then he would wake up, wonder where he was, and start whimpering all over again. It went on like this all night.

The next morning Robert came bounding down the basement steps before he went off to school. Joey was overjoyed to see him. He barked as loudly as he could and wagged his spindly little tail, and when Robert picked him up to cuddle him, he licked Robert's face as if it were ice cream. Mrs. LeClerc, however, wasn't so pleased. Joey had been to the bathroom several times during the night, and now she had to clean up after him. Getting the mop out of the cupboard, she realized that it was one thing to say that Joey was Robert's responsibility, but it was another to enforce it. What about when Robert was at school? Who would look after Joey then? It was something Mrs. LeClerc would have to discuss with her husband.

It was sunny again that day so while Robert was away at school and Mr. LeClerc was away at his office, Mrs.

LeClerc decided to put Joey out into the garden. That way, she thought, she wouldn't have to listen to him or clean up his messes. Joey thought this was a grand idea at first. There was so much to do in the LeClercs' backyard. There were plants to sniff and dirt to dig, and when he got tired, there was a large birch tree to curl up against. There were interesting sounds too: cars that trundled along the back lane; birds that chattered at him in the trees; and sometimes other neighbourhood dogs who barked. There was even a black cat who sat on the back fence and stared at him.

Even so, it wasn't long before he got lonely. He missed Robert. Yesterday, Robert had been there all day to play with him, but he was on his own today and he didn't like it. Suddenly, all the delights of romping about the trees and bushes and weeds no longer seemed so delightful. He wanted to go back inside where the people were. So he bounced over to the back door and started to scratch at it as best he could with his still blunt claws.

"Let me in, let me in," he yapped. But no amount of scratching and barking did any good. Though Mrs. LeClerc did open the door a few times, it was only to say "Shoo! Keep quiet!"

"Hey, what are you doing?" a voice asked as Joey went up to the door yet again. He turned around quickly, looked and sniffed, trying to figure out who had spoken. But he couldn't see anything.

"I said, what are you doing?" the voice repeated. It

wasn't a very friendly voice and Joey wished whoever was speaking would go away. But it didn't.

"Hey, can't you hear, Puppy?"

It was the black cat. She had appeared from out of nowhere the way cats do, and was sitting on the fence beside Joey.

"Yes, I can hear," Joey replied. Even though he didn't like the cat's voice, he decided he'd better answer. "I just didn't see you at first, that's all. Who are you?"

"My name's Marguerite. I live next door," said the cat.

"Hello," replied Joey a little nervously. "I'm Joey."

"So, Joey, what are you doing?" the cat asked for the third time.

"I'm trying to get back inside my house. My master's mother let me out and now she won't let me back in."

"Well, scratching at the door isn't going to help," meowed the cat. "You're just going to make the lady angry."

"Why?" asked Joey. "She loves me. They all do. They all wanted me. That's why they took me from the animal shelter."

"They may want you now," said the cat, "but they won't want you if you don't behave yourself. And barking and scratching at the door is going to make them angry."

"But it's my house too," said Joey. "Why would they be mad if I want to come inside my own house? Oh no, you're wrong. You'll see."

Joey began scratching again. He scratched so hard that

he scraped some of the paint off the back door. But no matter how hard he scratched, Mrs. LeClerc wouldn't let him in. Every time she opened the door, all she did was yell at him some more.

"See. I told you you'd only make her mad. But you wouldn't listen."

Joey didn't know what to think. He didn't want to make Mrs. LeClerc angry, but he wanted to get in the house. Now it seemed as if he might never be allowed inside again. Dejected, he went over to the large birch tree and sat down. He thought about what had happened and about what Marguerite had said, but he didn't want to believe it. Not now when the LeClercs were supposed to want him. At last, exhausted from so much thinking, he fell asleep, and for a little while his dreams took him away from his fears.

Meanwhile Mrs. LeClerc was getting fed up. She loved her husband and her son, but she enjoyed her time away from them too. She liked being in the house on her own and doing things at her own pace without interruption. But now, thanks to Joey, she was being interrupted all the time.

"I'm glad Robert has his dog," she told her husband later that evening. "And, of course, when Joey gets older, he'll be good protection against burglars. But who would have thought he'd be such a nuisance? Ever since we got him, he's done nothing but cause trouble."

"You don't know what it was like here today," she

continued, speaking more urgently. "All day long he was at that door scratching and yapping to get inside. Have a look at the marks he's left. He'd still be at it if Robert hadn't come home. It's not that I don't like him. You know that. He's a nice little dog. But this has got to stop."

"You're right, we will have to do something," agreed Mr. LeClerc. "We can't return Joey to the shelter, not when Robert is so fond of him. But we can't have you being so upset either. Perhaps the best thing would be to get him a doghouse and tie him up. That's what doghouses are for, aren't they? What do you think? Would that help?"

Mrs. LeClerc leaned over and gave him a kiss.

It was still winter but it was mild, so Joey would be fine, they told Robert. "And with spring and summer on the way, he'll be happy to be outside," Mr. LeClerc added. "After all, dogs are like wolves, right? And wolves live outside all the time. When you come home, you can let Joey off his leash as much as you want. You can even have him in the house providing there are no more accidents. But while you're away, Joey will have to be kept under control. We're sorry, but we have to be firm about this."

Robert just sat and listened. Evidently, this was going to be a long lecture, and he decided the best strategy was to stay still and say nothing.

"Keeping Joey outside will solve the problem of house-training him," Mr. LeClerc continued. "Remember the book the animal shelter gave us? It said a puppy couldn't be properly house-trained until he was five or six months old. Well, Joey isn't even two months old yet, so there's no way we can put up with him messing the house for three or four more months. But as long as he's outside, we won't have to. Understand?"

Robert nodded and said he did.

So Joey became an outside dog. The LeClercs bought him a long leash and tied him to a fence post. It allowed him to run fairly freely in the garden, but it wasn't long enough to allow him to reach the back door. They also bought him a brand new red doghouse for when it rained or was too cold for him to sleep outside. It had his name painted over the door. Robert liked that.

"You'll see, Joey," he said soothingly the first night Joey was kept outside. "You'll learn to like it out here. It'll be like camping every night."

Joey, who didn't know what camping was, pulled hard on his leash and howled when Robert left him. Then, remembering what Marguerite had said about making too much noise, he tried his hardest to keep quiet.

Left on his own in the garden hour after hour during the day, and then at night in the cold and rain, Joey grew more and more miserable. He wanted so much to go inside the LeClercs' house and be with his new family. He wanted to sit by their feet while they read the newspaper. He wanted to sleep on Robert's bed so he could alert Robert to anyone coming into the bedroom at night. And when they went out, he wanted to run with Robert, chase a ball with him, and play tug o' war with sticks.

But he never got the chance because Robert was away at school most of the day. When school was over, Robert had other things to do. There was his soccer team and computer club, and now he had begun to play little league baseball as well. Even when soccer season ended and he had more free time, he still had to have time to play with his friends. And Joey was still too young and unruly to join them. But Joey didn't understand that. He just felt left out. The only creature he had to talk to was Marguerite.

She came to see him every day. She would sit on the fence and look down at him while he chased back and forth on the end of his leash. Then when he got tired, he'd stop and talk to her.

"Why do you do that?" Marguerite asked, shaking her head. "Why don't you sit still like me?"

"Because I can't," whined Joey. "I don't know why, but if I sit still too long, I start to feel all funny inside. Even if I don't want them to, my legs want to get up and go, and I have to go with them."

"But you look so silly running back and forth on the end of that leash."

Joey didn't say anything. He thought Marguerite might be right, but he didn't want to admit it.

"And I think your family would be happier with you if

you sat still," Marguerite said. "They might even let you inside if you did."

"Really? Do you think they might? Then I will stay still! I will. I will."

But try as he might, he couldn't. His legs just wanted to go and go. So he kept running back and forth in the garden. Sometimes he grew so cross with the leash that he'd start to chew on it as if it were a bone. But the leash was strong and he never was able to bite through it.

Weeks went by like this, and Joey got bigger and bigger. And the more he grew, the more he wanted to run. But Robert was hardly ever around to run with him. Robert still loved Joey, but he had to admit that having a dog wasn't as much fun as he had thought it would be. It was a lot of work, just as his parents had said. They had to remind him to feed Joey and give him water, and although Robert was glad to see Joey and make him happy by feeding him, he got bored having to do it every day.

Even playing with Joey wasn't as much fun as he had hoped it would be. One day he tried taking Joey to the park, but it was a disaster. "Oh boy," Joey barked to Marguerite when Robert started to unhook the leash from the fence. "Look at me, Marguerite! I'm going out! You see, I'm finally going out!"

He was as excited as if it had been Christmas.

"Yes, I do see," said Marguerite, "and I'm glad. But

behave yourself," she added sternly. "Remember to do everything Robert tells you to do."

"What?" said Joey, who was too busy scampering about to pay attention.

"I said, behave yourself. Are you listening?"

"What?" But by now Robert had opened the garden gate and they were on their way out. "What did you say?" he barked.

"Never mind," Marguerite said to herself as she watched them go. "It's too late now."

All the way to the park, Joey pulled as hard as he could on his leash. It meant Robert had to pull just as hard in the opposite direction, and neither of them liked it. Then when they got to the park and Robert let him run free, Joey refused to come back when it was time to leave.

"Joey!" Robert called. "Joey, come back!" Then louder: "Come here right now!" He stamped his feet and shouted even louder, but still Joey wouldn't come. Finally Robert managed to sneak up on Joey and put the leash on him while Joey was busy digging after a mole. But then Robert had to fight with him all the way home.

Poor Joey was so confused. He couldn't understand why Robert was yelling or why he had to wear the leash. He would have followed Robert home without it. Robert should have known that. Joey just wanted to run and jump and sniff and roll over on the grass. He didn't want to be tied up. He was tied up enough. So he pulled just as hard on the leash going home from the park as he had on his way to it.

Robert carried on yelling even more.

"Robert, we think you should take Joey to obedience school," his parents said when Robert told them about the trouble in the park. "It really is time you learned how to control him."

"I will, I will," Robert promised. He agreed it was a good idea. But there was never any time. The classes always got in the way of his baseball practice or a computer fair or something else. So Robert suggested that Mr. and Mrs. LeClerc take Joey instead.

"No way," they both said. "Joey is your responsibility, not ours." So Robert never suggested it again.

And that's how things remained for four months. Joey was never trained, and the more time that went by, the bigger a problem he became. Bored and lonely, he began to tear up the garden. The LeClercs shouted at him when he uprooted one of their favourite plants, but their scolding always came too late so Joey never knew what they meant.

"Why are they so angry?" Joey would ask Marguerite afterwards. "What did I do wrong?"

Marguerite, who felt more and more sorry for Joey, just said: "Human beings are strange creatures who do strange things. You can't let it bother you." But it did.

Being left alone so much made Joey long for company. So he barked, hoping that someone would come along and make friends. "Please come and play with me," he barked. "Please come and play with me." But no one ever did.

All this barking drove Mrs. LeClerc crazy. Again and again she would yell at Joey to keep quiet, and for a few minutes he would. But then something — the sight of a stranger in the alley perhaps — would set him off again, and Mrs. LeClerc would have to yell some more.

The neighbours weren't happy either. They didn't like to complain to the LeClercs because they wanted to be on good terms with them. But when Joey's barking got to be too much, they had to say something. Then the LeClercs got angry with Joey all over again. If only someone had paid attention to him, things would have been different. But the more care and attention Joey needed, the less he received, until even Robert couldn't be bothered with him any more.

The last straw came when Joey was six months old. He was a big dog by then and with his upright ears and the handsome way he carried himself, he looked like a police dog. It was one of the reasons the LeClercs kept him. They were sure that with Joey tied up in the backyard, no burglar would dare set foot in it.

One day a little girl came with her family to visit the neighbours next door. She escaped her parents' attention for a few minutes and wandered through the gate into the LeClercs' backyard. She had seen Joey through the fence and was fascinated by him. "Here, big dog," she called to him. "Who are you? What's your name?"

Joey, who was excited to have company at last, ran toward her. "Hello," he yelped. "Have you come to play with me? We'll have lots of fun."

Joey's leash made it impossible for him to reach the girl, but even so, the sight of him barking and pulling at it terrified her, and she began to scream.

The LeClercs and their neighbours came out to see what the noise was about, and then they started shouting too. "Are you mad to keep such a dog?" the neighbours yelled at the LeClercs. "He could have killed her. He should be destroyed before he bites someone!"

The LeClercs knew Joey was no killer, but they also realized he had to go. Now they had to make Robert realize it too. "You know, Robert," said Mrs. LeClerc when they returned to the house, "Joey's been nothing but trouble since he got here, so we have to take him back to the shelter. We don't like to do it, but we have no choice. Don't worry, he'll find a home with someone else, but we can't keep him any more. Especially not after what happened today. You do understand that, don't you?"

"No!" Robert shouted. "I don't. Joey's my dog, and I don't want to give him up. No matter what those stupid neighbours say."

He carried on complaining right up until bedtime, and

it wasn't until his parents promised to buy him a new mountain bike that he calmed down and decided maybe they were right after all. He went to sleep thinking about what colour frame he'd like.

The next morning when the LeClercs came to get him, Joey thought they were taking him somewhere fun. But somehow Marguerite knew better, and before he left, she spoke to him more tenderly than she ever had before.

"Good-bye, Joey," she purred, rubbing up against him. "Look after yourself."

"Don't worry, I will," Joey replied, wagging his tail. "I'm going to have so much fun today. We're going to be one big happy family the way I've always wanted. You'll see. I'll tell you all about it when I come home."

Marguerite said nothing. She just brushed up against him again and nuzzled him a kiss.

When they got to the shelter, the LeClercs explained to Mr. McNulty why Joey was being returned so Mr. McNulty could judge whether Joey could be re-adopted.

"If he's bitten somebody, we'll have to destroy him," Mr. McNulty said.

"No, no, he didn't bite anybody. It was nothing like that," Mr. LeClerc said, deciding that it was best not to say anything about what had happened with the neighbour's little girl. "He's just not for us, that's all. Maybe another time and another dog. But right now, we think we're better off without any kind of pet."

"Too bad you didn't think of that before," said Mr. McNulty. "Is he trained at all?"

"You mean can he sit and stay and things like that?" asked Mr. LeClerc.

"Yes, things like that."

"No. We never got around to it."

"Didn't think so," said Mr. McNulty. "Is he house-trained?"

"No, we thought it best to keep him outside so there was no need."

"Not even house-trained," Mr. McNulty said, writing it down in a book.

"No," Mr. LeClerc repeated a little sheepishly.

"Well, we'll do our best." Mr. McNulty smiled an artificial smile. "But there are no guarantees."

"No," said Mr. LeClerc. Then he gave Mr. McNulty the leash they had bought when they decided to keep Joey tied up outside, put a small donation in the donation box, and walked out to his car.

"Sorry, boy," Mr. McNulty said to Joey as the LeClercs drove off. "Looks as if you're stuck with us again."

three

JOEY THOUGHT IT WAS STRANGE when Mr. LeClerc handed him to Mr. McNulty, but at least he was away from the garden, and he remembered what Marguerite had said about sitting still. So he decided to play it as cool as he could. But when the LeClercs walked out the door, an alarm went off inside him.

"No, no," he barked as he watched them go. "Don't leave me! I'll be good. Give me another chance. But don't leave me here, please!"

He tried to go after them, but Mr. McNulty had put a leash around his neck and it stopped him. It was a scratchy thing made of nylon rope with a loop at the end that fitted over his head like a hangman's noose. When Joey jerked forward, the noose tightened around his neck and made it impossible for him to bark properly any more.

Also watching the LeClercs go was a small, bright-eyed woman dressed in a bright red sweatshirt, jeans and red plastic gumboots. She stood near Mr. McNulty's desk so she could see the LeClercs' faces as they signed Joey over. When Joey choked himself on the leash, she rushed over to calm him down, stroking his head and speaking softly and soothingly to him.

"Poor Joey," she cooed. "What a terrible thing to do to such a lovely boy. Well, don't you worry, I'm going to work extra hard to find you a new home. A better home. A home where you'll be allowed to stay put."

Mr. McNulty finished filling out forms. He had to leave Joey tied up in order to get his work done, but the woman in the red sweatshirt stayed with Joey and kept stroking him. She told him again what a beautiful dog he was and petted his silky black fur. Then she put her arms around him and hugged him. She wasn't particularly strong, but she knew dogs and was good at handling them, even dogs as big as Joey was now.

"Worthless lot," she muttered indignantly to Mr. McNulty. She was a go-getter around the shelter and not one to mince her words. "How could they treat such a beautiful dog so badly? It makes me sick. A German shepherd cross with no training. And a black one at that. Do they have any idea how hard it will be to find him a new home? They probably don't care. They just waltz out of here and drive off in their fancy car and leave us to do all the work. It makes me sicker than sick." She almost spat the words out.

"Yeah, I guess so," replied Mr. McNulty. He was used

to Marjorie grumbling about people who were cruel to their dogs. She always got worked up about it. But after ten years of working at the shelter, he had pretty much seen it all, so he no longer got angry the way Marjorie did. He felt sorry for the dogs, and it made him unhappy to see people treat them badly, but once the dogs were safely in their cages, he tried his best not to think about them.

"Would you put Joey in a cage for me?" he finally asked when he finished filling out the papers. "You're familiar with the dogs, Marjorie, so you know which ones he'll get along with. Then let me know where he is, so I can enter it in the book."

"All right," Marjorie said, still angry. "But I still think that family's worthless." Then, in a much sweeter voice, she said to Joey, "Come on, darling. Come with me." Marjorie liked German shepherds more than any other kind of dog, and even though Joey was a mix, he still had that proud German shepherd look that Marjorie loved. Though she tried her best to treat all the shelter dogs equally, she couldn't help having favourites.

Joey liked Marjorie too. Kindness was something he had had too little of at the LeClercs'. But he didn't like the rest of what was happening. For one thing, he wasn't used to the other dogs. He had seen dogs go by the alley behind his house and had heard them barking from a distance, but he was never allowed to make friends with them. So even though he was curious, he was wary too.

And the dogs he saw inside the cages looked miserable. Some of them didn't bother to get up as he was led by, but most barked wildly at him, and some wrapped their teeth around the criss-cross metal strips of the cage doors, and growled.

"Hey, who are you?" these dogs called out. "Did your owners leave you alone, too? Well, don't expect it to be easy in here. Don't expect anything at all."

They all sounded so angry and unhappy that Joey couldn't bear to listen to them or think he was one of them now. What was to become of him, he wondered. What was to become of all of them? He just wanted to lie down and cry, but he forced himself to be brave, and barked back, "Keep quiet. Leave me alone!"

When they didn't stop, he cowered on the ground to show them he didn't mean any harm. Then Marjorie had to pull even harder on his leash to get him to move. Joey hated that. It hurt when the noose tightened, and he fought every yank. He didn't want to be one of these crazy caged dogs. Even being tied up in the LeClercs' backyard was better than this.

At six months old, Joey was still a puppy, but he was far too big to go in the puppy cage. Instead he had to go into one of the adult dog cages. Marjorie thought carefully about which dog to put him with before deciding on Mick, also a German shepherd cross, but a year older than Joey and with gold instead of black fur. Mick was a good-natured animal, and Marjorie was pretty certain he wouldn't fight with Joey, but she wasn't as sure of Joey. She didn't know how he would take to other dogs. Unless the dog's previous owner had said something about how his dog got along with other animals, the only way to find out was to put the dogs in together and see what happened. Usually they got on pretty well, but Marjorie had seen a few fights in which one or both dogs had been badly hurt.

Each of the shelter cages was divided in half by a metal flap that Marjorie could raise and lower as she wished. One side of the cage faced outside onto a courtyard, and the other faced inside onto a long corridor. At night all the dogs were herded into the inside halves to keep them warm. Though the cage floors were hard and uncomfortable, they were heated at night so that even in winter the dogs didn't freeze. But during the day, and especially in spring and summer, the flaps were kept open so that the dogs could use both sides of their cages. This gave them a bit more room in which to move, and it allowed them to look at the people and animals who passed by.

Mick's cage was at the end of the courtyard, and he, like most of the other dogs, had his nosed pressed hard against the outside cage door sniffing and staring at the small world outside. He barked as Joey was led closer, but Marjorie wasn't worried. By now she could tell the difference between an angry bark and a friendly one, and Mick's was full of cheer. In fact, when she and Joey stopped outside Mick's cage, Mick stopped barking altogether. But his ears were pricked high with interest, and his nose was working furiously.

Joey looked inside the cage and shuddered. It was so small, no bigger than a garden shed. There was just enough room for him and another dog to turn around in, and its walls were hard and grey. He didn't want to go in. But hard as he pulled, Marjorie pulled even harder. She sure wasn't being the sweet, soft-spoken lady she'd been in the shelter office, he thought.

She clanged the cage door shut with a terrible noise. Still, at least Joey wouldn't be alone.

"Hello," barked the dog. "I'm Mick. What's your name?"

"Joey," Joey replied nervously. Mick sounded friendly, but Joey was so unaccustomed to other dogs that he remained on his guard. What if Mick wanted to fight with him?

But Mick didn't. He just sniffed Joey all over, and then sat back on his haunches.

"Don't be afraid," reassured Mick. "I don't want to fight. We might have to spend a long time in here together so we may as well be friends."

Joey didn't reply, but he felt better.

"Most of the dogs in here feel that way," Mick said. "We're all in the same mess so we may as well not fight amongst ourselves."

"But the other dogs looked so angry to see me."

"They weren't angry," answered Mick. "They were just bored and you were something new for them to look at. It happens every time someone goes by. The only thing there is to do in here is sleep, but you can't sleep all day, so when you wake up, you look for something to take your mind off your troubles. And today it was you, that's all."

"But some of them looked as if they wanted to bite me," Joey said, "the way they were biting and chewing their cages."

"They just wanted to get out," Mick said. "They saw you outside their cages so they wanted to be outside them too. Some of us have learned that biting doesn't do any good, the walls are too strong to tear down. But others keep trying. I don't know why, but they do. There was a dog in the next cage who bent his paw badly when he tried to shove it under the door. He had to go to the hospital to have it treated. I don't think he'll try it again."

It all sounded terrible to Joey, but from the way Mick spoke, it appeared as if he didn't mind it too much. He had such a cheerful, friendly face, and there was only kindness in his voice.

"Aren't you unhappy in here?" Joey asked.

"I don't like it, that's for sure," Mick said. "But I figure I may as well make the best of it. If I wait long enough, maybe someone will come along to adopt me. And I know Marjorie likes me."

"Who's Marjorie?" Joey asked.

"She's the lady who brought you in here. She's always coming in here to look after us. You'll like her. She's one of the nice ones."

Mick was a special favourite of Marjorie's. She loved walking and brushing him every chance she got, and she had high hopes of finding him a good home. She was more than a bit puzzled that he hadn't found one sooner.

"Who are the not nice ones?" Joey asked, afraid again.

"Some of the guys who work here don't seem to like us much," Mick said. "I don't know why, but they don't. Some of them are okay, but they don't pay us much attention unless they're feeding us or cleaning our cages."

At that moment, Joey and Mick heard a loud noise coming from outside the cage, and they, along with the rest of the dogs, ran to the cage door to see what it was. One of the shelter workers, who didn't like his job or the dogs, was passing in front pretending to hold a machine gun. As he jerked his arms up and down as if he were firing a real gun, he made a rat-a-tat-tat noise. It was something new for the dogs to look at, and most of them, including Joey, jumped up and started barking.

"See," said Mick. "Sometimes they do things like that, but none of us knows why. Don't let it bother you."

But it did bother Joey. It was just as Marguerite, the cat, had said: humans were strange creatures who did strange things.

It was a mercy that Joey had somewhere to go when

the LeClercs abandoned him, but he still thought the shelter was an awful place. Just as Mick said, all he did was sleep because there was nothing else to do. But he didn't sleep soundly. Usually, he had bad dreams. If the dream was too frightening, he would wake up, barking loudly enough to wake Mick up too.

"Hey, Joey," Mick would say. "What's wrong?"

"Nothing," Joey would answer. "Just bad dreams." But he felt embarrassed. He thought he should be braver than that.

Then he and Mick would get up, turn around a few times the way dogs do, and try to get comfortable again. But it wasn't easy on that floor. Mick had already developed a sore on his skin from rubbing it against the hard surface.

"Hey," said Joey, noticing the rough spot for the first time. "What's that?"

"You get it from sleeping on these floors," Mick said. "Mine isn't too bad, but you should see some of the other dogs. They get so crazy being in here that they start to bite and scratch at their own fur. Sometimes they even pull it out, and the red, raw patches left behind get infected. It's awful."

There also was the problem of filth. Mick had been house-trained, but being penned up all day meant he couldn't hold it back. Joey, who had been kept outside at the LeClerc's, didn't know he shouldn't go to the bathroom indoors, but he knew he didn't like having to walk and lie down in his own mess. That was horrible. But as long as he and Mick were kept inside, there was nothing else they could do until a shelter worker came along to clean up. Sometimes they had to wait hours for that to happen.

There were days when Joey didn't think he could stand it another minute. On these days, he would post himself at the cage door and howl like a wolf baying at the moon.

"Keep quiet!" Mick would yell at him when he did. "Remember, the shelter workers don't like dogs who make a fuss. They think they're trouble-makers."

"So what? What happens to those dogs?" Joey asked Mick one day as they both set about eating the crumbly, sludge-coloured food that was put in their cage every day at noon.

"They're taken away," Mick said, chewing a mouthful.

"Where to?" Joey asked, not remembering the stories Blackie had told him when he was still a very young pup.

"I don't know," Mick answered. He swallowed. "I just know that sometimes dogs are taken away and never seen again. Sometimes a family comes and takes them away, but sometimes they just disappear. You see all those people who come by the shelter every day to look at us?" Joey had. "Well, sometimes those people adopt dogs."

"I remember," Joey said sadly. "That's how I met Robert."

"Right. Well, that's how Ginger, the cocker spaniel in

the next cage, got a home yesterday. But there are never enough people to give homes to all of us, so sometimes dogs have to disappear."

Joey gulped nervously. Slowly, memories of what Blackie had told him long ago — unpleasant memories about the dangers of not being wanted — returned to him. And here he was, five months later, in the same danger. Except now it was worse because he was older and bigger. He remembered what Blackie had said about people always wanting young pups instead of older dogs.

"How do they decide which dogs disappear?" Joey whispered.

"The sick ones go first, so whatever you do, don't get sick. And stay away from other dogs if you hear them coughing because if you don't, you might catch what they have."

"I will," Joey promised. "But what's wrong with them?"

"They get kennel cough," Mick said. "It's like a cold. It makes it hard to breathe and you cough a lot when you have it. I had it when the people I lived with put me in a kennel for a week when they went on holiday."

"How did you get rid of it?" Joey asked, amazed that Mick was still alive to tell the tale.

"I went to the vet, the dog doctor, and he gave my master some medicine to give to me, and it went away in no time. It isn't a big deal."

"They why do dogs disappear if they get it?"

"Because it spreads so easily, especially in a place like

this," Mick replied. "It's like a stain. It starts out small, but then it gets bigger and bigger, until soon all the dogs are coughing, not just one. And that's when dogs start disappearing."

"But I still don't understand," Joey said. "It's so unfair."

"But it's the way it is. Around here they don't think anyone would want to adopt a sick dog. Maybe they're right. We healthy dogs have to wait long enough to find a home. So whatever you do, don't start coughing," Mick repeated.

"I'll try my best," Joey promised, and meant it.

"Then if there are no sick dogs, the old ones are taken away," Mick continued. "That's why it's a good thing you're only six months old, because if you were six years old, you'd have a much worse chance. In fact, you might have disappeared already."

Joey gulped again. Everything Mick was telling him sounded so frightening that part of him didn't want to hear any more. But another part wanted to know the full story.

"Then there are the fierce dogs," Mick said.

"Which ones are those?" asked Joey.

"They're the ones who bite and snarl at people, so don't ever do that," Mick warned.

"I won't," Joey replied. "But if it's so bad to bite and snarl, why do the fierce dogs do it?"

"They can't help it. They were trained that way. Their owners wanted them to be guard dogs so they taught them to be fierce. It happens a lot to dobermans, rottweilers and pit bulls. Pit bulls have it the worst. They're trained to fight each other, but when the people don't want them any more, they're brought here."

"And then what happens?" Joey asked.

"Sometimes kind people adopt them and teach them not to be fierce any more. But usually the staff take them to the back where they ..."

"Disappear," interrupted Joey. It wasn't hard to guess.

"Afraid so."

One morning not long after their talk, five dogs left their cages and never came back. Joey and Mick watched them as they went, frisky and trusting, hopeful of finding a home. But Joey worried that they might have been taken away to disappear instead. He didn't know which dogs were sick or old or fierce. All of them looked fine to him. It was up to the shelter workers to decide, and remembering the man who had done the weird thing with his arms, he wondered what went through their minds.

Unlike Mick, who had decided to make the best of a bad situation, Joey worried all the time. He also felt as if he would explode sometimes for lack of space. While Mick would lie quietly in a corner half asleep, Joey, with his puppy's energy, would pace back and forth like a crazed lion in a zoo. He would bark at nothing, sometimes just a change in the light would set him off. Mick would tell him to keep quiet because he didn't want him to become known as a trouble-maker, but sometimes Joey couldn't stop. Then an angry shelter worker would yell "Shut up!" It meant he was getting to be known as a difficult dog.

Once when it was time for a worker to hose down the cage floor, Joey refused to budge. Mick went quietly to the back to be out of the worker's way, and told Joey to follow. "Come on," he urged. "Don't make the man angry."

But for some reason — not even Joey knew what it was — Joey stayed put. The worker shouted at him, but Joey still refused to move. So the worker turned the hose on full blast and soaked him. The water was cold, and the force of it made him sputter and bark. But it also made him move to the back of the cage — at last.

"Why did you do that?" Mick asked when Joey was safely out of harm's way.

"I don't know," said Joey, still sputtering. "I couldn't help myself."

The worker looked at Joey and shook his head.

Joey didn't like the food he got either, and though he usually finished his bowl, many of the other dogs didn't. A small dog held in the cage next to Joey's was afraid of getting close to his food dish because of his bigger, stronger cage mate. Another dog farther up the row of cages was so unhappy just to be in the shelter that she hadn't eaten in two days. Whatever the reason, it was rare for a shelter dog not to lose weight. And even if they had a shine on their coats when they came in, it wasn't long before it dulled and disappeared. It had already begun to happen to Joey's coat. Mick's too.

However, there was a point in the day that Joey did enjoy. All the dogs did. It came early in the evening when Marjorie and a crew of fellow volunteers arrived to walk them. The volunteers were a raggle-taggle bunch. Some were young, some old. Some drove Jaguars, some rode bicycles. Some were as fit as runners, some hacked like smokers. But they all liked the dogs and wanted to do their best for them.

They took them to a park across the road. There, they would run around a jogging path or zig-zag across the grass from one end of the park to the other, and back again. There were no rules except that the dogs were to be kept under control and on leashes at all times. But sometimes if a volunteer were walking a dog he or she could really trust — a dog the volunteer knew wouldn't run away — he might break the rule and let the dog run free for a while to chase a ball or stick. Marjorie let Mick free, and he loved it, even if it was for just a short while.

"Ho, ho," he would cry as he ran down the field with the wind in his face and the sweet, soft grass under his feet. "This is the life!"

Sometimes he chased flocks of seagulls resting on the grass, and they would rise in a rush, screeching and swirling over his head.

"Keep quiet, you silly dog," they would caw. "You run

too fast and you make too much noise."

But Mick didn't care. He felt as if he could run forever.

As well as keeping the dogs exercised and happy, walking them was supposed to keep them used to people. That way, when the time came for them to be adopted, they wouldn't shy away from their new owners. Instead, they would wag their tails, bark a cheerful hello, and be happy to be on their way. At least that was the plan.

The length of the walks depended on how many volunteers there were. In winter when only a few hardy souls arrived in their parkas and rainboots, the dogs were lucky to get ten minutes each. But as it was summer, there were lots of volunteers to help. It meant that for an hour every evening Joey was set free from the cage he hated, and allowed to see and feel the world outside it. How he loved that hour — to feel the sun on his face and back, to step on the soft ground instead of the hard concrete, and to sniff the trees and flowers to his heart's content.

"I wish we never had to go back," he would say to Mick again and again. "I wish the walk could go on forever and ever."

There was only one thing about the walk that Joey didn't like — the leash he had to wear. When he pulled too hard on it, its noose would tighten around his neck and choke him. But even it couldn't spoil his enthusiasm for being outside. Nothing could do that. The moment the volunteers arrived, Joey would be up like a kick, barking "Me first! Me first!" with all the other dogs. Even Mick, who usually was so calm and dignified, would leap to his feet and join the clamour. He and Joey often were taken out together, and whenever possible, Marjorie took Mick.

Marjorie had four grandchildren, but she was as lively and energetic as they were. And sometimes, like her grandchildren, she would come home with a cut over her eye or a pair of skinned knees from where she had been knocked over by an especially large dog. It drove her husband crazy. But it didn't bother her. She loved helping the dogs too much to ever give it up.

Still, she wasn't as strong as she once was, so she often let the younger volunteers walk the bigger, stronger dogs. But Mick was so well trained that Marjorie always walked him. She tried walking Joey too, and did her best to keep him under control, but sometimes he would pull so much that she had to give him to another volunteer. When the cage door was opened, Joey would roar out of it like a train. The tightening noose kept him from running away, but he still would pull hard on it, forcing the volunteer to dig in his or her heels and pull hard in the other direction. But Joey wasn't stupid, and after a while, he began to realize that such tug o'wars were pointless. More than that, they hurt. Gradually he learned to behave himself, and that, Marjorie knew, was sure to improve his chances of being adopted.

He also began to enjoy other dogs, now that he knew

they didn't mean him any harm. He liked to play and rough-house with them, and though this made holding onto him even harder, the volunteers were glad to see him happy.

"Hey, Mick," Joey would call when he did something to make a volunteer proud of him. "Look at me."

"You're getting the hang of it, Kid," Mick would call back. "Just stick with it and you'll be great."

"As good as you?" Joey barked.

"Better," promised Mick. "You'll be one in a million."

Mick already was one in a million. He was pure joy to everyone who knew him. He had been left at the shelter by a couple who were getting divorced and weren't able to look after him any more. Marjorie couldn't understand why one of the splitting partners didn't take Mick. However, they had looked after him while they had him, and had taught him to obey all their commands. It meant he would walk at whatever pace Marjorie wanted. Slowly, quickly, or at a full run, he was always beside her. He also sat and stayed when she told him to, and he took biscuits from her as gently as a deer.

"You see that?" Marjorie would say to Joey after Mick had done something especially well. "Why can't you be more like Mick instead of such a trouble-maker?"

But she always said this with love in her voice. As the days passed, she had grown more and more fond of Joey, and because she had had German shepherds of her own, she knew all about dogs like him. She thought he was handsome, and she liked what she called his "sticky-up ears". His coat had lost its lustre and his fur had grown tatty, but Marjorie had seen Joey when he first came in, so she knew how beautiful he could be. It was simply a matter of finding someone to adopt him. So even though Mick was her first love, she paid special attention to Joey too. She hugged him, called him "Chum," and always fed him biscuits. She promised herself that the moment she had found a good home for Mick, she'd start working on one for Joey.

It turned out that might be soon. Marjorie had spoken to a couple on the phone about Mick, and they had promised to drive in and meet him as soon as they could arrange it.

Later, Marjorie told Mick all about it. She always spoke to the dogs as if they could understand.

"Mick, my boy," she said, "it won't be long now before you're on your way. Just think, at long last you'll be able to say good-bye to this place. Won't that be grand?"

Then she rolled him over on his back and rubbed his tummy. Mick loved this, and rolled back and forth from one side to the other hoping Marjorie would never stop.

"I know your pal will miss you," she continued, reaching over to pat Joey's head. "But he'll get over it, and then we can get busy finding him a home."

"I don't know, Mick," Joey said later when they were back in their cage.

"You don't know what?" Mick asked patiently.

"I don't know how I feel sometimes. I mean, I really, really want to get out of here."

"Who doesn't?"

"But I also hate the idea of saying good-bye to you. When the volunteers take us out, we have so much fun together. I don't know what I'd do without you."

"I know," said Mick, "but when the time comes, you'll learn to love the people who adopt you too. And who knows, maybe some day when we're both out of here and living with good families, we'll meet in the park and play tag or chase a ball together. That'll be great. But we'll probably have to remind ourselves of what it was like in here because we won't remember. Who knows, when the time comes, maybe we won't want to remember. Maybe it will be just like that."

"I hope so, Mick," Joey replied. "Because you're the best friend I've ever had."

Marjorie wouldn't rest until the people who were supposed to adopt Mick had signed the papers and taken him away. She was sure they'd love him. He looked so handsome with his broad, grinning face, his deep brown eyes, and his golden fur shimmering in the sun. And he was such a gentleman too, always doing exactly as he was told. If only they'd hurry up and meet him.

Finally, an appointment was made, and Marjorie promised Mick that the couple would be along to see him in just three days.

But that night after all the shelter lights had been

turned off and the dogs were locked in their cages, Joey woke up to a strange sound.

"Hey, Mick, was that you?" he whispered to his friend.

"Was what me?" Mick answered, a little annoyed. "Go to sleep."

"No, I heard a noise," Joey said. "Did you make a noise?"

"I don't know what you're talking about," Mick said. "I didn't hear anything. Go back to sleep."

"Well, if you say so, but I could swear I heard something," Joey replied.

He settled back down again, but as soon as he closed his eyes, he heard the noise again. And this time he was sure it came from Mick. So sure that he rose to his feet as quickly as if someone had hit him.

"Mick!" he shouted. "That *was* you, wasn't it? That was a cough. Mick, have you got kennel cough?"

four

"SHSH!" WHISPERED MICK to Joey before he could bark again. "Don't make so much noise. Do you want one of the shelter workers to hear you? Because if he does, he might hear me, and neither of us wants that, right?"

"No, sorry," Joey whispered back. "But Mick, I'm worried. You've got kennel cough, and you told me that dogs with kennel cough …" He couldn't make himself say it.

"Disappear." Mick said it for him. "I know, and that's why I've got to be careful and not attract attention to myself. And you've got to help by not attracting attention to either of us. Maybe if we can keep it quiet long enough, it'll go away and there won't be anything to worry about."

"Really? Do you think so?" Joey asked, full of hope again.

"I don't know," Mick said. "But I do know I feel fine except for the cough, and even that's not too bad now.

So maybe if I hide in the back of the cage when the shelter workers come by and try my best not to make a sound, they might not notice it. It's worth a try."

"I promise to be quiet," Joey said, his heart beating like a hummingbird's wings. "I promise not to cause any more trouble. I'll do anything if it means that you won't … disappear." Saying the horrible word made Joey feel sick, as if his insides were filled with prickles. "They can't take Mick away," he thought to himself. "What would I do without him?"

Thoughts like these jabbed at him all night. Somehow Mick managed to sleep, but Joey tossed and turned like a boat in a storm. Each time he drifted off to sleep, he was awakened by Mick's coughing. To him, it was like thunder. It got so he expected an army of shelter workers to turn up at any moment wondering what the noise was. And as the night wore on, it got worse.

"Mick, how are you? Are you better? Do you think it's going away?" he badgered his pal the next day.

"I don't know," Mick said. "I feel fine; it's just that every once in a while I feel like …" A cough interrupted him. "Doing that," he finished.

"But how did you get it?" Joey asked. "You told me we had to be careful not to get it."

"I know I did. And I thought I was. I don't know how I got it. But last night when we went for our walk, I felt a tickle in my throat. I thought it would go away, but it got worse. And now, well, you can hear how bad it is."

"Oh Mick," cried Joey, "what are we going to do?"

"I told you last night," Mick said. "We're going to be as quiet as possible and hope no one hears us. And one other thing, Joey, we're going to keep you healthy. So whatever you do, don't come too close to me. I know that's going to be hard in such a small cage, but you have to try. I'm going to stay at one end of the cage, and you're going to stay at the other. Okay? Got it?"

"Got it," Joey said. "I will."

So he did. When one of the shelter workers came by to open the flap that led to the outside half of the cage, Joey rushed through it as fast as he could. Some of the other dogs in the shelter began barking when their cage flaps were opened, but Joey kept silent, remembering what Mick had said about not attracting attention to them.

The morning passed slowly. Mick coughed some more, but no one heard him. A shelter worker walked by the cage once or twice, but he never stopped to look inside. Joey and Mick knew, however, that the real test would come at feeding time. Then the shelter worker would be right inside their cage with them, and one cough could make the difference between staying and disappearing.

The food arrived at noon. Because Joey and Mick's cage was the last in the row, they were always the last to be fed, but today they didn't care. Neither of them was hungry. Joey wondered if he would ever be able to eat again.

"Okay, you guys," the shelter worker said, making the usual scraping sound as he set the metal tray down on the concrete floor. "Here it is. Come and get it." Then he stood over the tray and waited for Joey and Mick to start eating. "Hey, your food's here," he said when neither dog came forward. "Aren't you hungry?" He waited a few moments more for one of them to begin, but when neither did, he shrugged his shoulders and gave up. "Well, it's here if you want it," he said.

He opened the cage door and was about to take a step outside when Mick couldn't hold it back any longer. He coughed.

"Mick!" Joey barked. Then he started to bark and bark and bark hoping the shelter worker would pay attention to him instead. But it didn't work.

The shelter worker knelt down close to Mick and took a long look at him. "Are you all right, fella?" he asked. "Was that a cough I heard?"

Mick was scared to death of making another sound, but he couldn't help himself. A second cough leapt out as if it had a will of its own.

"Yep, that was a cough, all right," said the shelter worker. "We'll have to see about that." Then he turned around and walked out the cage door, locking it behind him.

"Mick," Joey cried when the worker was gone. "He's gone! Maybe he doesn't care that you coughed. Maybe it's all right. Maybe he'll give you some of that medicine your old owners gave you. Maybe we were worrying about nothing."

"I don't know," Mick said quietly. "Maybe, but I was told by the other dogs when I came in here that if you coughed, you disappeared. It was the rule. I hope you're right, Joey, but I don't know."

So they waited. For one hour. Then two. Then three. And still nothing happened. Mick kept on coughing. Occasionally a worker would stop by to listen, but otherwise they left him alone.

"You see, Mick, I was right. They don't care. If they did, they would have been around long ago. But it's been hours since we were fed and you're still here."

Just at that moment, a pair of large black boots appeared at the cage door. They belonged to the same shelter worker who had doused Joey with the hose when Joey had refused to move, and he had a leash in his hand.

"Sorry about this," he said as he opened the cage door. "But we can't risk all of you getting sick."

Then he walked over to Mick and put the leash around his neck. As soon as he did, Joey started barking and snarling so violently that it seemed he would go for the worker's throat. But Mick told him to keep back.

"Don't, Joey!" he barked and coughed. "Don't make it worse for yourself!"

Joey kept on barking. "No, Mick. I've got to stop him! I've got to stop him from taking you away!"

But the shelter worker ignored Joey and led Mick out the door. They went quickly, but as he went, Mick managed to jerk his head around to look at his pal once more. "Good-bye, Joey," he said as bravely as he could. "Good-bye. Look after yourself and don't forget me."

Joey choked back a whimper, shook his head and promised that he never would.

When Mick was out of sight, Joey turned around slowly and looked at their cage. He could picture Mick as clearly as if he were still there, grinning at him with his big, doggy grin and scratching behind his ear with his hind foot. He could hear Mick's voice too, giving him advice or just chatting with him about what life had been like before he got to the shelter. They often spent their days doing that. He imagined Mick at the cage door wagging his tail the way he used to when it was walk time. Mick sure loved his walks. Joey loved them too, but Mick was a changed dog when he was out in the park. In the cage, he was a perfect gentleman, never causing trouble for anyone. But outside, he showed what a spirited dog he still was, running and chasing and carrying on like a puppy. Joey loved seeing him that way.

But now he was gone, and Joey felt sure he wouldn't see him again.

Joey sat and thought about that for a long time. He didn't even want to go on his walk when the time came.

The volunteer had to coax him out, and worried he might be sick. But knowing what happens to sick dogs, she didn't dare say anything; she just stroked him, gave him some water and eventually got him out for a couple of spins around the park. Afterwards, Marjorie stopped in to say hello, and because she was special to him, Joey appreciated the way she put her arms around him to comfort him.

Marjorie took Mick's death hard. When she first saw Joey alone, she had misunderstood what had happened, and assumed that someone had come in off the street to adopt Mick that day. So she ran to the shelter office where the adoption records were kept, and asked Mr. McNulty to let her know who the person was.

"I want to call and tell them what a great dog they've got," she said, delighted at the thought of Mick finally being out of his cage. "I know it's against the rules, but I want to know what kind of people they are. Mick was such a great dog; he deserves someone special."

But when she looked in the record book, there was no adopter's name beside Mick's name, only the letters HD which stood for Humane Destruction. It was how the shelter referred to killing a dog.

Marjorie was shocked. "Wait a minute," she said, "this can't be. It says HD next to Mick's name. But no one could have put him down."

"Sorry, Marjorie, but he had kennel cough," Mr. McNulty said. "And you know the rules."

"Yes I do," Marjorie said trying her best to collect herself. "But even so, you couldn't have done it. Not to Mick. Surely you had more sense than that."

"Sorry, Marjorie," Mr. McNulty repeated, "but you know the rules. And we can't make exceptions."

"But he was a perfectly adoptable dog," Marjorie shouted. "In fact, he was a perfect dog in every way, and I had people coming this weekend to look at him. They would have taken him with or without kennel cough. All it takes is a few pills to cure it. You can't have put him down. You just can't have done!"

"Sorry, Marjorie," Mr. McNulty said a third time. "We don't like it any better than you do."

"Well I'm sorry, too," Marjorie said furiously. "Because this is wrong, and I am going to make sure someone knows it!"

She went to see the shelter's director, Mr. Forrester, to tell him what happened and demand that it never happen again, but he said the same thing Mr. McNulty had. "Rules are rules," he told her over his desk in his office, "and much as we would like to, we can't save every dog. It's a sad fact of life around here. You know that as well as anyone, Marjorie."

"Yes, I do," Marjorie said, barely able to control her anger. "But this is different. If only you or your staff had paid him some attention, you would have realized what a special dog Mick was. You could have given him a few pills and he would have been as right as rain in a week or so. Right?"

"Marjorie ..." Mr. Forrester said.

"Well?" she interrupted him. "Am I right or not?"

But she realized there was little point in carrying on. She had heard everything Mr. Forrester had said a dozen times before, and nothing she said could change his mind. Nor would it bring Mick back.

But this time she had had enough, she decided. She left the shelter, promising herself she would never come back. It was too heartbreaking, and she wasn't going to beat her head against its concrete walls any more.

Try as she did, though, she couldn't stay away for long. Other volunteers phoned to ask where she was, and each time they did, she had questions about the dogs. After a week, she gave in. "True, Mick is gone," she told herself bitterly, "but there are other dogs too. And I'm not going to be able to do much for them sitting around here. Besides, there's Joey to think about. I couldn't find a home for Mick, but I'm going to find a home for Joey if it kills me."

By the time Marjorie returned to the shelter, Joey had been there over a month. It was a long time by the shelter's standards. Marjorie knew this, but she wasn't going to let it stop her. No matter what happened, she wasn't going to let the shelter put Joey down. She'd made up her mind.

"You've got your work cut out for you," her friend Jane said as they ran the dogs around the park that night.

"You know they think that once a dog's been here longer than a month no one will want to adopt him."

"I know," Marjorie said, "but I don't care. I'm going to find a home for Joey."

"Good luck. But you know how people can be. Joey's a big dog, and people always want little dogs to sit on their laps."

"I know, I know," sighed Marjorie, "you don't have to tell me."

"They want purebred dogs too," Jane said. "If they can get them."

"Isn't that amazing?" Marjorie exclaimed. "Those dogs cost five hundred dollars and more. You wouldn't think someone would dump a five hundred dollar dog in an animal shelter, would you? But luckily for them, they don't stick around long."

"If only Joey weren't black," Jane said. "He'd have a much better chance of finding a home if he were white or tan or even brown. Anything but black. No one ever wants a black dog like this." She leant over to pat the black dog she was walking and give her a biscuit.

"I know," Marjorie said, petting her own black dog. "I'm almost tempted to paint him another colour."

"He's not even trained," Jane added. "That's going to make it really hard to find him a home."

"Listen, Jane," Marjorie said. "Are you deliberately trying to make me feel bad? Because if you are, you're doing a heck of a job. I know he's black and I know he's big and I know he's not trained. Is there anything else?"

"It's summer," Jane replied.

"Oh, thank you," Marjorie said sarcastically. "Yes, to top everything off, it's summer. And we all know that no one ever wants to adopt an animal in summer."

"No. People go on holiday in summer, and they leave their pets behind. I just wish they wouldn't leave them behind with us."

"I know things will improve in September when the kids start going back to school and everyone settles down again," Marjorie said, "but what am I supposed to do about Joey until then?"

She and Jane ran a little farther around the park, petting their dogs as they went.

"I don't care," Marjorie suddenly said, picking her spirits up. "I said I was going to find Joey a home, and I will. I'll find him a good, caring responsible home where he will be looked after for the rest of his life."

"Good luck," Jane encouraged, smiling. "'Cause you're going to need it."

Every Saturday and Sunday afternoon, Marjorie, Jane or one of the other volunteers arrived at the shelter to show the dogs to visitors. They were just like used car salesmen, they said. But instead of inviting customers to kick tires and slam doors, they would offer them the chance to take a second-hand dog out for a spin.

The volunteers knew how easy it was for people to overlook a dog cowering in a corner or barking desperately to be set free. They knew the dogs were at their worst in the cages, but could change as if by magic once they were let out. All they needed was a chance, and the volunteers were there to give them one.

But dogs like Joey — big, black untrained dogs — needed an extra push. So the next time it was Marjorie's turn to "move those dogs," as she called it, she was going to make sure he got it.

"Come on," she would say to people who came in looking. "Come meet Joey. He's a grand fellow. Friendly, full of life. If you can call living in here life. How about it? Maybe he's the dog for you." Sometimes Joey would stand up and wag his tail right on cue as if he understood what Marjorie was saying.

It didn't work, but occasionally, even though they didn't take Joey, people adopted other dogs, and Marjorie always was pleased when they did. After all, she was there to move all the dogs, not just one. She also was careful to make sure that the adopters were people the dogs could trust. She talked to them for a long time so they would know exactly what they were getting into. She wanted them to value and love their dogs until old age or sickness ended the dogs' lives. "It's just as the bumper stick says," she said to them. "A dog is for life, not just for Christmas."

But it didn't do any good for a volunteer to be at the shelter to talk to people if there were no people to talk to. To make sure there were, Marjorie placed advertisements for the dogs in the local newspaper. When people answered the ads, she explained that the dogs were kept at the animal shelter, but that she knew them as well as if they were her own. Sometimes people made appointments to meet her and the dogs when they heard that. It was how she had found the couple who were supposed to adopt Mick.

The ad she placed for Joey read: "Friendly, frisky, seven-month-old German shepherd cross, male, needs a loving home urgently. Good with children and other dogs. Please help."

Marjorie was able to say Joey was good with children because he had lived in a home with a child. And she knew he was good with other dogs because she had seen how he had played with them on his walks.

She waited almost ten days for the first reply, and when it came, it wasn't good news.

"I want a guard dog," the caller said. "My place has been broken into a coupla times, and from the sound of your ad, your dog might be what I'm looking for."

"Maybe," said Marjorie, "but I'm afraid that kind of home is not what I'm looking for. I'm looking for someone who wants a pet, not protection. In fact, I'd rather see this dog dead than tied to a rope his whole life."

"Why you ..."

But Marjorie rang off before the caller could finish.

The next reply wasn't much better. This caller wanted a small dog.

"But the ad said German shepherd cross," explained Marjorie. "That's a very large dog."

"Is it?" asked the caller, not at all embarrassed. "Oh. Well, have you got any small dogs?"

Marjorie explained about being a volunteer at the animal shelter and told the caller to go there and look for herself.

The third reply was more encouraging. The caller knew what German shepherds were because he had had one before. More than that, he had two acres of property outside the city where Joey would be able to run free to his heart's content. Marjorie's spirits soared. This was just what she was hoping for. But her hopes were dashed when the caller said he was going on holiday for a month and wouldn't be able to look at Joey until he got back.

"Sorry," the caller said.

"So am I," Marjorie replied. But she took his name and telephone number anyway because she knew that in a month there would be an equally needy German shepherd cross looking for a good home.

The fourth call was like the first. The person wanted a large dog to guard his warehouse. He explained that Joey would be there alone with the watchman at night, but during the day he would get lots of attention from the daytime workers. Marjorie wasn't too sure about it, but time was running out, and it was better than nothing. But the caller got mad when Marjorie told him the adoption fee the shelter charged was to pay for having

Joey neutered.

"There's no way, lady, that I'm going to allow that to happen to a dog of mine," he said. "It's not natural."

"Then good-bye," Marjorie said. She had nothing more to say to him.

Joey had no idea that any of this was going on. All he knew or cared about was that he was still locked up twenty-three hours a day. It had been seven weeks since he had been brought to the shelter, but he still remembered what life had been like outside of it. He got a taste of it every evening during his walk, and the longer he was denied that life, the more he wanted it.

After Mick disappeared, Joey had stopped his frantic pacing and spent more time lying on the concrete floor. However, he always remained watchful for anyone passing, and when someone did, he'd leap to his feet and bark madly. This annoyed the shelter staff since it usually was one of them passing by. But this time Marjorie had told them about her plans for Joey, so the staff overlooked his bad behaviour. They liked Marjorie, and didn't want to upset her any more.

"But you know, Marjorie," they warned her. "We can't keep Joey alive forever."

"No," Marjorie said, "but I can."

Success, or what Marjorie hoped would be success, came a few days later. "My husband and I had a dog who died two months ago and we're ready to adopt another one," the lady who called said. "We saw your ad for the German shepherd cross, and we'd like to know more about him."

"My pleasure," replied Marjorie. "His name is Joey, and he's big and — I'm afraid — completely untrained. Well, maybe he'll sit if you tell him to, but not much else. But he's very friendly and eager to please and, I'll be frank with you, in desperate need of a good home."

"Oh, we don't mind if he's large," the woman said. "In fact, we prefer large dogs. Our dog who died was a black labrador, so we're used to big dogs. And it doesn't matter that he's not trained because we trained our last dog ourselves. We don't mind a challenge. Who knows, Joey might be just what we're looking for."

"I hope so," Marjorie beamed. "It would be wonderful if he were."

She was over the moon with relief. She had begun to wonder if she would ever find Joey a home, but it looked now as if all her patience and hard work had paid off. The couple, Mr. and Mrs. Spencer, agreed to meet her the next day, Saturday, to have a look at Joey and take him for a walk. They also promised it wouldn't take long for them to make up their minds. They said they knew dogs and were sure of what they wanted, and it sounded to them as if Joey would fit their bill.

So that evening when Marjorie took Joey out for his walk, she made a special point of brushing him from head to tail. His coat wasn't anything compared to what it had been when he arrived at the shelter, but Marjorie thought a bit of brushing wouldn't hurt. It would make a good impression on the Spencers, and she wanted everything to be just right.

"You wait and see, Chum," she said as she tugged at the knots in his fur, "tomorrow is going to be your lucky day. If everything goes the way I hope it will, you'll never have to spend another night in that horrible cage. Won't that be nice?" She held his chin and moved his face near to hers. "Aye, Chum? What do you say to that?" Then she hugged him and started to laugh when he barked at her, as if he'd understood what she'd said.

It was warm and sunny that evening so a lot of volunteers showed up to walk the dogs, including a young teenage boy who had never been to the shelter before. The other volunteers were glad to see him since everybody's help was welcome, and the boy seemed eager enough. First he took one dog, then another and then Joey.

But by the time he got to Joey, he was getting bored. He wasn't much of an animal lover, he decided; all he'd wanted was something to do that night, but now he realized that walking dogs wasn't it. He'd rather have a cigarette. So after tying Joey's leash to a lamppost, he sat down and lit one, and as he dragged on it, he began to think of other things.

Joey was annoyed. "This is supposed to be my walking time, not his sitting time," he thought. "I do enough sitting in the cage all day."

He was so annoyed that he started to pull on the leash, and when he did, the knot the boy had tied came undone. It was hardly a knot at all, just one loop under and over, so it came apart easily. And when it did, Joey was free for the first time in seven weeks.

He was so used to being on a leash that at first he didn't know what to do. But then it hit him. "I'm free," he thought to himself. "I'm really free. I don't ever have to go back to that cage again, and what happened to Mick will never happen to me."

He began to run. First he ran around the park barking at the other dogs and the volunteers, and yelping with joy. The boy dropped his cigarette, ran after him and tried to catch him. But Joey was too fast for him and everyone else. Marjorie shrieked when she saw what had happened, and called Joey over and over hoping he would come to her. Joey was fond of Marjorie and it was all he could do not to obey. But he just couldn't go back inside that cage. Not even for her.

So with Marjorie, the boy and all the volunteers calling him to come back, he ran up a hill and into the setting sun, like a cowboy in a movie. He stopped long enough to take one last look at the shelter, the dogs and the volunteers, but then he was on his way. He didn't know where he was going, but he didn't care. At long last he was free.

"Good-bye, everybody," he barked as the dogs and people grew smaller and smaller. "Good-bye and wish me luck." When they were completely out of sight, he stopped to catch his breath and drink in his freedom. It tasted great.

"Are you with me, Mick?" he asked, looking up at the sky. "Are you coming with me?" He paused for a moment to listen for an answer. Then, satisfied that he had one, he turned on his heels and barked, "Then let's go, Chum. Let's you and me see the world!"

five

JOEY'S FIRST TASTE OF FREEDOM was like a tonic. He hadn't felt so good in weeks. The whole world was open to him, he thought. He could go wherever he wanted, whenever he wanted, and no concrete walls or wire mesh doors would hold him back. He knew he would miss Marjorie, but after what had happened to Mick, he didn't want to go back, no matter what.

At first he ran around just for the sake of it, going in this direction, then that, then another, just to prove he could go anywhere he chose. Sometimes people would give him funny looks as if to say, "What are you doing out on the street on your own without a leash?" It had dropped off his head soon after he'd run from the park. But he hardly noticed them. People weren't his business any more, he decided. From now on, he would make it on his own.

It had been so long since he had been allowed to run like this that he didn't stop 'til the dreadful soreness in his legs that came from being held in that tiny kennel finally began to ease. However, as it was summer, all that running made him thirsty. At the shelter there always had been two buckets of fresh water put out for him, but out here he didn't know where to turn. It hadn't rained for days, so there weren't even any puddles about, though he looked everywhere for one: in people's gardens, in back lanes and in carports.

"What am I going to do?" Joey wondered. "I have to find something to drink."

The more he worried, the more over-heated and thirsty he became. He started to despair when finally he spotted some water leaking from an outdoor tap. He rushed over hoping to quench his thirst, but the drip was very slow and he only got a little at a time. It was better than nothing, but it sure didn't compare to the long, cool drinks he got at the shelter. He missed those.

Joey stood at the tap for several minutes lapping up what little water he could, when a slamming door and an angry voice startled him.

"Hey," bellowed the voice. "What do you think you're doing? Get outta here, you mangey mutt!"

The voice belonged to a fat, red-faced man wearing jeans, cowboy boots and a black T-shirt. Joey stood up straight and started to bark at the man, but his barking made the man even angrier.

"Shut up!" the man yelled. "Shut up and get outta here before I kick you out!"

Then the man took the beer can he had been drinking from and threw it at Joey. He missed, but some of the beer flew out and splattered Joey's face. Joey leapt back, but kept on barking. He didn't know what else to do.

"Okay," growled the man, the anger rising in his voice. "Maybe this'll get rid of you." He picked up a large block of wood and came at Joey, holding the wood over his head like a club. This time Joey did run. He ran as fast as he could, and kept on running long after the man was out of sight.

Several blocks away he stopped when he saw a dog tied up in another garden. It was a large, black dog with upright ears like Joey's. But his eyes were lifeless, and he had a strange look on his face. But Joey was so glad to see a dog, any dog, that he didn't notice. He ran closer, wagging his tail and smiling his widest smile.

"Hello," he barked, his voice full of cheer and relief. "I'm so glad to see you. Can you tell me where I can get a proper drink of water?"

"What?" growled the dog, starting to bare its teeth. "What did you say?"

Joey was startled by the dog's growl and thought about running away. But he still hadn't had enough to drink and his thirst got the better of him.

"I said, do you know where I can get a drink?"

"Get out of here! Get out of here! Get out of here!" The dog barked so fast that all his words ran together like gunfire.

Joey was as surprised as he had been when the man had thrown the beer can at him.

"Get out! Get out! Get out!" the dog hollered. The strange thing was that he didn't seem to know what he was saying. Trained as a guard dog, he was more like a machine than a living thing.

So Joey ran away again, feeling even more alone than before. He began to realize that being free also meant finding food and water, and now that the sun had gone down, somewhere to sleep too.

At first he tried making himself comfortable in another backyard where there were no dogs or people, but when the owner of the backyard looked out his window and saw Joey, he chased him away. Another man did the same thing when Joey tried to sleep in his garden, so Joey learned quickly that such places were off-limits. But since most of the neighbourhood was made up of houses and gardens, what was he to do?

He walked around in the dark, tired, thirsty and unhappy, not knowing where to turn. He even thought of heading back to the shelter — he was fairly sure he could pick up its scent — but changed his mind. "No, Mick," he said, looking up at the canopy of stars that filled the night sky. "I don't want to disappear. So I can't go back there. But I don't know where else to go. People keep chasing me out of their gardens. Help me, Mick. What should I do?"

Perhaps he hoped Mick would guide him to a place

where he would be comfortable and welcome, but no such place appeared. He was even chased out of a public park by a gang of teenagers who were out late drinking. "Hey, you get outta here!" one of the teenagers yelled when Joey came toward him. Some of the teenagers were scared of him, while others just wanted a lark, so they shook their beer cans and sprayed Joey with the foam that spewed out the open tops. Joey yelped when the spray hit him, and he ran away.

At last, after hours of searching, he found an empty schoolyard with a covered play area. There was no one about, so he finally was able to lie down and curl up. But the blacktop surface wasn't any more comfortable than the shelter cages had been, and after all he'd been through, he decided to sleep with one eye open in case someone else appeared to chase him away.

It didn't take much to wake him the next morning. A group of young boys was passing through the schoolyard on their way to play baseball, and their laughing and joking put Joey on guard. At first they didn't notice him because they were too busy playing catch and taking practice swings with their bats. But then one of the boys saw Joey and ran over to him.

"Hey guys, look at the dog," the boy called out to his friends. "I wonder who he belongs to."

Joey, who was alert to every sound now, was ready to flee. He was all set for this boy to throw something at him or drive him away. But this boy was different. When he was a few steps from Joey, he stopped running and started to walk quietly toward him.

"Hi, boy," he said to Joey in a calm, friendly voice. "How ya doin'? Where do you live? Where's your owner?" As he said this, he moved forward until he was directly in front of Joey. Joey remained on guard, but even so, he sensed that this boy was friendlier than the teenagers had been. He even allowed the boy to put a hand under his chin and stroke him along his back. He liked the boy's touch and the sound of his voice.

"Hey boy, what's your name?" the boy gently asked Joey. "Don't you have a tag or something with your name on it? You should have." Then he noticed the shelter tag that Joey still wore, and read out the number on it. "Sixty-seven. What kind of a name is that? Is that your name, Sixty-seven?" The boy started to laugh, which made Joey bristle nervously again, but the boy was fine. "Okay, Sixty-seven," he laughed. "That's what I'll call you then."

"Hey, Mark," one of the other boys called. "Get over here and leave that dog alone. We want to play."

"In a minute. I just want to say good-bye to ol' Sixty-seven first."

"What?" asked the other boy.

"Never mind," said Mark. "I'm coming." Then he turned back to Joey, gave him one last pat on the head, and said: "Good-bye, Sixty-seven. I wish I could have you for my dog, but my mum won't let me. Besides, someone must be looking for you. You better go back to him."

When Mark ran off to join his friends, Joey was tempted to follow. His was the first kind voice Joey had heard since he left the shelter. But seeing Mark's friends made Joey nervous. After the run-in he had had with the teenagers the night before, he was wary of groups of children. Instead, he wandered off in the opposite direction to look for something to eat.

Following his nose to the nearest garbage, he detected something edible. But the garbage was wrapped tightly in a plastic garbage bag, and as soon as Joey started to rip it, a woman came tearing out of her house. "Get out of here!" she screamed, just as the others had done before her.

But Joey was still hungry, so he tried another garbage can. This one wasn't tied as neatly, and he was able to grab a few scraps of chicken before he was chased away again. Sometimes the smell of a thrown away food wrapper would lure him. He would hold the wrapper on the ground with his paws and lick off whatever crumbs were left. Once in a while there was even a bit of bun left inside or a few french fries. He would gobble them up hungrily. But it was never enough.

He hadn't liked the food in the shelter, but at least it had always been there. And he had always looked forward to the biscuits Marjorie gave him when she took him for a walk. But where was she now? Where was anyone who could help him find something to eat?

"Hey, you," hissed a voice as Joey began to paw at another heap of rubbish. "Get away from here. This is my place, not yours."

By now Joey was used to being chased away from places, but this time the voice wasn't human. He stopped what he was doing, looked up and saw a scrawny cat sitting and spitting on the fence above him.

"I said, get away from here," the cat hissed again. "That's my food you're trying to take."

"Sorry," Joey apologized. "I didn't know it belonged to anyone."

"Well, it does," snarled the cat, who jumped down and took a swipe at Joey's nose with her long, sharp claws. She missed, but Joey wasn't about to risk tangling with those claws again, so he stepped back quickly.

"It's mine," said the cat. "Everyone around here knows that."

"Really?" Joey asked. "Who's everyone?"

"All the wild dogs and cats. Who else?"

"Wild dogs?" he thought to himself. "Is that what I am?" Then he said to the cat, "Sorry, I didn't know there were any other wild animals here. I thought I was alone."

"Well, you're not," spat the cat. "There are others around here who need to eat, too. So leave my food alone."

Then the cat started to pick at the garbage that Joey had strewn over the pavement, and nibble at anything she could find. She ate quickly and furtively as if she expected to be disturbed at any moment.

"Where do the other animals live?" Joey asked, wishing the cat would allow him to eat something too.

"Here and there," said the cat. "Everywhere. They live everywhere."

"But I didn't see any animals 'til I saw you," Joey replied.

"That's because we're smarter than you," hissed the cat. "We know how to hide. You have to know how to hide if you're going to survive out here."

"But where?" asked Joey. "Where do you hide?"

"You have to figure that out for yourself. It's not every animal who can make it on the streets. You've got to be tough and quick and smart. Are you tough? You don't look tough."

The cat looked like a veteran of a hundred fights. Her fur was thin and ragged. She had sores on her back near her tail, and one of her ears had a triangle-shaped nick out of it from where an enemy had come too close with a claw.

Joey didn't know what to say. He wasn't sure if he understood what the cat meant.

"I guess so," Joey replied. "I guess I'm tough."

The cat stopped rooting through the garbage and started to make a cackling sound like a laugh. "You don't look tough to me," she said. "You look like you'd be better off with humans. Why don't you try and find yourself a home somewhere with humans?"

"I did," Joey said, "but the humans didn't want me. So then I went to the animal shelter, but nobody there wanted me either, so I escaped."

"Ah, the animal shelter," said the cat. She was interested in that. "The men in blue shirts tried to take me there once, but I wouldn't let them. I was too slippery. So they gave up. There's no way I'm ever going to go to that place 'cause I know what happens to cats there."

"Dogs too," exclaimed Joey. "It happened to my best friend, Mick. He started to cough one day and they took him away. That's why I escaped. I didn't want them to take me away as well."

"Hmmm," said the cat. "Maybe you're smarter than you look. But you've got to learn the rules out here, and one of them is to keep to your own territory. And this territory is mine."

"Okay, I will," promised Joey. "But where do I find a territory of my own?"

The cat cackled again. "That's up to you, my friend. That's up to you."

"Hey, Cookie, don't be so hard on him," chuckled another voice from behind. "He's new at this, so don't scare him too badly."

The voice belonged to another dog, about two-thirds the size of Joey, with a striped brown and black coat, and a large head sitting on powerful shoulders. But the rest of the dog was as thin as a stick. And like the cat,

Cookie, he had rough, red patches on his fur.

"Shut up, Dumpster," said Cookie. "I'm just showing this greenhorn the ropes. You know as well as anyone that it's the law of the jungle out here: only the fit and strong survive."

"Yeah, yeah," said the dog. "But I say give the kid a break. How are ya?" he said to Joey. "I'm Dumpster. I'm what you call a pitbull cross. What's your name and what kinda dog are you?"

"My name's Joey," Joey replied a little shyly. "And I'm a German shepherd cross."

The dog started to grunt good-naturedly. "Yeah, we're all crosses out here, that's for sure. Ya won't find any of those fancy, high-toned purebred types wandering the streets like us, aye? No, it's a mutt's world out here."

"He escaped from an animal shelter," informed Cookie.

"No kiddin'," replied Dumpster. "So ya broke outta jail, did ya? Well, whaddya know?"

"I've been out one night," Joey said. "I ran away during my walk. Last night I slept in a schoolyard and today I've been looking for food."

"Well, then, we gotta find ya some," Dumpster said, grinning from ear to ear. "You're a hero in my book. Ya got guts, kid. So stick with me. I'll show ya how to get around. We'll be a team, okay? Whaddya say?"

"That would be great," Joey said. He was relieved. Dumpster was someone who knew his way around the streets — someone who would know where to find water and forage for food and most important, how to stay away from angry men with beer cans.

"Are you sure?" Joey asked.

"'Course I'm sure. I gotta feelin' about ya. From now on it's you 'n me against the world, and we'll beat it, aye. We'll have a great time. I'll show ya all the best places to get food and water, and I'll show ya where to put your head down so's nobody will bother ya."

After all he had been through, Joey couldn't believe his luck. Maybe now, he thought, with Dumpster's help, he would learn how to live by himself and he wouldn't ever have to worry about going back to the animal shelter or finding a home with humans again. He couldn't wait to begin.

"So where do we start?" Joey asked eagerly.

"Right here," Dumpster replied, "with lesson number one. Ya gotta respect other animals and their privacy. Bein' dogs, we like to travel in packs. But cats are different. Most of the time they like to be by themselves. Ya can try chasin' 'em, but sometimes they got awful mean claws and ya don't wanna risk gettin' scratched on the nose when you corner 'em. That can hurt like nothin' else. So it's best just to keep outta their way. And remember: this here is Cookie's way. Okay?"

"Okay,"

"Okay, then," Dumpster said. "Now I'll show ya where we go."

And with that, he took off down the lane with Joey in

tow. They didn't travel far, just a block or two, but it seemed even a short distance could make all the difference in the animal world. In the shelter, there were no such things as territories, but then in the shelter many of nature's laws were bent or broken. Here on the outside they mattered again.

"Did ya see the scars on Cookie?" Dumpster asked. "She got 'em protectin' her territory, just like we gotta protect ours," Dumpster said. "Those are the rules, okay?"

"Okay," Joey replied.

"As long as ya understand. Now, whaddya say we find somethin' to eat?"

"Great," Joey said. He was still famished and he couldn't wait to find some food.

"I know a place nearby where people are always chuckin' out good stuff to eat. Come on, I'll show ya."

The place was a tipped-over garbage can full of unwrapped rubbish, and what food scraps there were, were open to whatever stray animal wanted them.

"Here we are," Dumpster said, pleased with himself. "Now dig in."

"What's the matter?" Dumpster asked a few minutes later. He had been licking the Styrofoam trays clean, enjoying every swipe his tongue took across them, and only now saw that Joey wasn't quite as enthusiastic. "Ain't there somethin' to suit your taste?" he asked, teasing. "Listen, Kid, when ya live on the street, ya gotta

take what ya can get. Nobody puts fancy dog food out for us here. Ya eat what ya can find, and if ya can't find somethin', ya keep on lookin' 'til ya do."

Joey agreed. It wasn't that he didn't like the scraps. He was hungry enough to eat anything. It's just that it made him sad to realize that now he would have to search for food every time he was hungry. Before he'd always been given his food. The LeClercs had always fed him well, and even though he hadn't liked the shelter food, at least he didn't have to go looking for it. Out here on the streets, life seemed to be one big battle for food, water and a place to sleep, and Joey was beginning to like it less and less.

Still, he ate what he could find and was grateful. It wasn't much, that was for sure. No wonder Dumpster was so thin. The shelter dogs had been thin too, but not like this. Then Joey noticed Dumpster's tail. It was gnarled and bent in the middle like a broken twig on a tree in winter.

"Dumpster," Joey said, "what happened to your tail?"

"Huh?" Dumpster said, looking up from his food. "Oh, that. It got hit by a car. Ya gotta watch out for cars out here. That's another thing I gotta tell ya. Ya never know when one is gonna turn up from outta nowhere. Usually, I'm pretty good at avoidin' 'em, but this one got me. I still don't know how 'cause I swear I was runnin' as fast as I could. But sometimes it happens."

"Didn't it hurt?" Joey asked.

"'Course it hurt. It hurt more than I ever thought anythin' could. It also didn't heal right — that's why it's bent — but it healed. And it don't hurt hardly at all no more. But that don't mean ya shouldn't watch out, 'cause ya should. Let me tell ya: If the men with sticks don't get ya, the cars will. So don't forget it."

Joey promised he wouldn't.

They spent the rest of the day looking in other places for food. Sometimes they would find some; sometimes they wouldn't. Once they got lucky when a little girl got so frightened by the sight of them that she dropped the hamburger she was carrying and ran away. It was an unexpected feast.

"Ya don't often get this lucky," Dumpster said, licking his chops. "So enjoy it while ya can."

Even so, there wasn't much for two hungry dogs to share, and Joey didn't feel very lucky. Slowly he was beginning to realize that living on the streets meant always being hungry — as if someone were poking him in the stomach with a stick. He wondered if it ever got so you didn't feel the stick any more.

"'Fraid not," Dumpster said. "It's your hunger that keeps ya on your toes. It also keeps ya movin' because you're always on the lookout for another meal. I told ya that when ya live this way, ya gotta eat what ya can find when ya can find it. 'Cause if ya don't, you're gonna starve."

They spent the night in a construction yard not far

from where they met Cookie. Dumpster said they were lucky to get it because usually such yards were boarded up. There was a fence around this one too, but one of its boards was loose enough for Dumpster and Joey to push aside and crawl past.

"Ain't this great?" Dumpster asked Joey when he showed it to him.

"It sure is," Joey replied, trying to sound pleased. But the truth was that it didn't look any more inviting than the schoolyard had. Boards and nails were strewn everywhere, and the ground was rough and gravelly. He couldn't see any place to sleep, but Dumpster said every place was as good as the next. And for the night, at least, it was all theirs.

"But when the sun comes up, we gotta get outta here lickety split, 'cause that's when the workers get back," Dumpster warned. "And there's no tellin' what they'll do if they see us. They might like dogs, but they might not. And when you're a stray, ya don't take no chances."

Then he lay down against a pile of construction boards and shut his eyes.

"Good-night, Joey," he mumbled before falling asleep. "Glad to have ya aboard."

"Good-night, Dumpster," Joey responded. "And thanks." But Dumpster was already snoring. It wasn't often that a stray dog gets to sleep soundly, but here in the construction yard it seemed no one would bother them, so Joey decided to follow Dumpster's lead. He didn't realize how tired he was until he curled up on the gravel and closed his eyes.

The next day was much like the one before. Joey and Dumpster searched for food and water, and tried to stay out of trouble. Sometimes they had no choice but to venture into somebody's backyard to get a drink. As long as there wasn't any rain, leaking taps were their only sources of water. Joey hated drinking from them, remembering only too well the man who had chased him away with the club. But Dumpster said as long as he was careful, there was no reason to be afraid. "If ya get caught, run," he added. "Don't bark or try to stay your ground. Just run."

Back at the construction yard, Dumpster asked Joey if he thought he was getting the hang of things.

"Oh yeah," Joey answered, trying to sound as streetwise as his new friend. "But I was wondering: Isn't there any time to play?"

Dumpster stared at Joey for a moment or two, not believing what he had heard. Then he sat on his haunches and roared so hard that he almost choked. "Play?" he jeered. "Ya gotta be kiddin', Kid. There ain't no time for play. Ya gotta spend all your time tryin' to stay alive, and even then ya don't live too long. How long do ya think the average stray lives out here? Go on, guess."

"I don't know. Ten or twelve years?"

Dumpster started to laugh again. "Ten or twelve

years?" he cried. "Boy, have ya gotta lot to learn. It's more like ten or twelve months, and that's if you're lucky. Some don't make it ten or twelve days. How old do ya think I am?"

"Five or six years old, maybe."

"I'm a year and a half," Dumpster said. "That's just a few months older than you, ain't it? But out here, that's old. If ya live with people in a good home, ya can live a long, long time — ten or twelve years like ya said. But not out here. Out here if the cars don't getcha, somethin' else will. But hey," he said, trying to sound more cheerful, "it's how ya live, not how long ya live, right? And out here we live on the edge, and as far as I can tell, that's the only way. Agreed?"

"Agreed," Joey said, but only to please Dumpster. After only two days, he knew he didn't want to live this way any more. He didn't want to live at the shelter either, but at least there he had a chance of finding a proper home with a good family. That, Joey realized, was what he wanted most: a family like the ones he and Mick talked about — a family who would take care of him. And if that meant going back to the shelter, that's what he would do.

The next morning Joey decided to tell Dumpster about his plan. He didn't know how or when to bring it up because he didn't want Dumpster to be disappointed in him. He let the morning pass and part of the afternoon before he finally gathered the courage to say something.

"Dumpster," he began after they had finished scratching over one pile of garbage and were about to sniff through another one. "Can I talk to you about something?"

"'Course ya can," Dumpster said. "But can ya talk while we move? I hate to stop once I've got goin'."

"Oh sure," Joey said, still trying to sound cool. He didn't want to upset Dumpster any more than he had to, and began to follow his friend to the end of the alley where it met the main road. With each step he tried harder and harder to say what he wanted to say, but he was still nervous about how Dumpster would react.

"What's on your mind?" asked Dumpster.

"Well," Joey began, "it's like this…" But before he could say any more, there was a piercing screech of tires as a car roared into the alley entrance. It was travelling so fast that it almost rolled over, and it moved far too fast for Dumpster to see. It made a terrible thud when it hit him, and it didn't even stop when Dumpster fell to the ground.

Joey barely escaped being hit too, and when the car drove off, he ran to see if Dumpster was all right. He'd heard the horrible sound the car made when it hit Dumpster, but maybe it wasn't as bad as it sounded.

It was.

Dumpster was dead. Joey sniffed him all over to make sure, and then lay down beside him. His body was still warm, so it was almost as if he were sleeping, not dead.

But he wasn't breathing, and there was no life in his eyes.

Joey was so sad he almost couldn't stand it. He didn't want to believe that his friend was gone. Not so soon after Mick. Why was it, he wondered, that no sooner did he learn to love someone, than that someone disappeared? First Robert, then Mick and now Dumpster. Is that what it would always be like? He didn't have an answer, so he just lay there next to Dumpster feeling sorry that life hadn't turned out better for him or his friend.

He stayed that way until a truck arrived from the dog pound to collect Dumpster's body. As soon as Joey heard the truck, he ran off and hid behind a fence. He'd had enough of cars for one day. Besides, it was time to return to the shelter. Now that Dumpster was dead, there was nothing to stop him. He lifted his nose into the breeze to search for the shelter's scent, and when he was satisfied that he had it, he began running. And he kept on running back to what he reckoned was his last and only hope.

six

IT WAS LATE AFTERNOON when Joey got back to the shelter. On the way he had stopped to wonder if he was doing the right thing. Remembering what had happened to Mick, he was afraid the same thing might happen to him, especially now that the shelter staff were bound to consider him a trouble-maker. But thinking about Dumpster made him realize there was nothing else to do. What he wanted was to live in his own home, and the only way he was going to do that was if someone adopted him from the shelter. At least he knew Marjorie would be glad to see him.

She was. She cheered when she saw his face appear in the doorway, and dropped her handbag as she rushed over to greet him.

"Joey!" she cried. "You're back! I'm so glad to see you!"

Then she flung her arms around him and hugged him close to her.

"Where have you been, you naughty boy?" she asked.

"You scared me to death. I thought you'd been hit by a car. Oh, you are naughty," she said again, but with such tenderness that Joey could never have guessed she was scolding him.

When she had patted and stroked him some more, and given him some dog biscuits, she did what she hated to do — put a leash around his neck and led him out to the cages. But she knew she had no choice, not until someone came to adopt him. Joey's heart sank when he saw all the dogs penned up again, and he felt sick when Marjorie opened the door to an empty cage. For a second, he even thought of escaping again, but he knew now that bad as this was, it was the only place left.

Marjorie stayed with him while he took a long drink of water and ate more biscuits. He was so glad to have them that he almost gobbled her fingers along with the food. But Marjorie didn't mind. She knew Joey wouldn't hurt her or anyone else. She just laughed and said, "Make sure to give my fingers back when you're finished with them." Then she stroked him again and brushed his coat.

Until then Joey didn't realize how exhausted he was. But now that he was safe in the shelter, all he wanted was to sleep. He wouldn't even mind the concrete floor as long as no one came after him with a club or a beer can.

"See you, Joey," Marjorie said on her way out the cage door. "Be good. And if you let me, I'm going to find you a proper home this time. Just don't run away again."

That night she phoned Mr. and Mrs. Spencer, and told them Joey was back. At first they weren't too keen to meet a dog who might run away from them, but Marjorie convinced them that it was the young volunteer's fault and that once Joey was in a stable, responsible home, he wouldn't stray again.

"Okay," said Mrs. Spencer, "we'll give him a chance, but only on your say so."

They arranged to come the following Saturday at noon. Marjorie almost couldn't wait for Saturday to arrive, and when it did, she came an hour early to give Joey an extra walk and a brush. She wanted him to be as calm and well-behaved as he could when he met the Spencers, and she wasn't about to take any chances.

Now that Joey was more accustomed to walking on a leash, Marjorie could walk him without anyone else's help. Even so, the walk probably tired her more than it did him, but at least he was trying to behave himself and not pull her around the park like a sled dog. It was a start, she thought.

The Spencers arrived while she was brushing Joey's back. Joey had loved the walk, and even though he wasn't too pleased with the no-nonsense way Marjorie was attacking the burrs in his coat, he trusted her and was enjoying the attention. So he really was at his best when the Spencers greeted them.

"Hello, Mr. and Mrs. Spencer," Marjorie said. "I'm

Marjorie — we spoke on the phone — and this (she gestured toward a still well-behaved Joey) is Joey. He's just having his coat brushed after his, well, after his little adventure."

The Spencers laughed and said he looked very good despite everything.

"You should have seen Jack, our lab, after a run through the woods on a rainy day," Mrs. Spencer laughed. "Sometimes we'd go through two towels getting the mud off of him."

Marjorie liked the Spencers straight away. From the way they spoke and handled Joey, they appeared to be people who knew about animals. After chucking him under his chin, and stroking him along his chest and back, they took him out for a long walk, during which they did their best to carry on his training. They even tried to make him sit on command. He wouldn't, but they said they weren't worried. "That and everything else will come," Mr. Spencer said.

Joey liked them too. He could sense they were dog lovers by the way they spoke to him and touched him. They weren't afraid of him either. In fact, they made it clear to him in a short time that if he did go home with them, they would be in charge. He resisted that at first, but then realized it might be for the best. Joey needed a pack leader, as long as it was someone kind and loving, and the Spencers appeared to be up to the job.

"Please take me," Joey barked at them once he had

made up his mind he liked them. "Please take me home and see how good I can be. You won't be sorry."

Marjorie shushed him and told him not to bark so much. The Spencers wouldn't like it, she said.

"That's okay," Mrs. Spencer reassured her. "He's just excited, aren't you, Joey?" She tucked her hand under one of his ears and gave it a rub. Then turning to Marjorie, she added: "You were right, he is a nice dog, almost exactly what we were looking for." Joey looked up at her, smiled in the way that dogs can, and wagged his tail. "But you were right about him needing to be trained."

"Yes, but he's at just the right age for training, and German shepherds are very smart dogs," Marjorie said as encouragingly as she could. She wasn't about to put the Spencers off now, not when things looked so promising.

"Oh, we realize that, and as we told you on the phone, that isn't a problem," said Mrs. Spencer. "I'm sure that in a few weeks he'll be fine. All it will take is a firm hand and lots of TLC."

"That means you want him?" Marjorie asked as calmly as she could, even though her heart was taking off like a rocket. "We'd be so pleased if you did because poor Joey has been here a long time, and we're getting a bit worried about his future." She decided to be cautious and spare them the gory details about putting dogs down.

"I think we do," said Mr. Spencer, "but we'd also like

to look at some of your other dogs before we make up our minds."

"Oh, I see. Then go right ahead," encouraged Marjorie, even though she didn't want them to. For while it was true that she wanted all the shelter dogs to find homes, she wanted Joey to find one first.

Nonetheless she decided to remain hopeful and leave Joey out of his cage. Perhaps, she prayed, he wouldn't have to go back into it. The Spencers said they liked him, and Mrs. Spencer had promised on the phone that she and her husband were people who made up their minds quickly.

But Marjorie's hopes were dashed with their next request.

"May we take Snowy for a walk?" asked Mr. Spencer. Snowy was a beautiful white Samoyed who had been brought to the shelter the day before. Her owner had to give her up because she was moving to a place where dogs weren't allowed.

"Certainly," Marjorie said, her spirits sinking fast. Joey was her own special pal, but she knew that in the adoption stakes, he wasn't in the same league as Snowy. She was the sort of dog the shelter seldom saw for long: a pedigree female with the kind of sunny looks that made dog lovers want to drop their parcels in the street and run over to say Hi.

Joey, however, knew none of this. He loved being with Marjorie; he loved being outside his cage; and he had no idea the Spencers wanted to look at another dog. He just wished they would hurry up and take him for another walk. So he began to pull hard on his leash.

"Sorry, Chum," said Marjorie, rubbing the top of his head so his ears began to dance. "I'm afraid I've got to put you back in your cage now." She didn't want to, but with the Spencers taking such an interest in Snowy, there was nothing else to do.

Joey couldn't believe what was happening. Did this mean the Spencers weren't going to take him? It couldn't, he thought. So he stood his ground and refused to budge no matter what Marjorie said or how hard she pulled. Marjorie had to ask another volunteer to help move him, and even then it took some doing to put Joey back in his cage. He barked angrily the whole time. But when the door was shut and locked, Joey knew he was beaten.

Meanwhile, Snowy was busy melting the hearts of Mr. and Mrs. Spencer. Marjorie had been right: Snowy was irresistible. Not only was she beautiful to look at, she was beautifully trained. Like Mick, she was an older dog who sat and stayed on command, and she walked on a leash as proudly and perfectly as a show animal. The Spencers would have been crazy not to take her. Of course, they apologized to Marjorie for changing their minds about Joey and wished her luck finding a good home for him, but after taking Snowy for a walk, there had been no contest.

Marjorie smiled and said she understood. She was even

pleased to see Snowy adopted. The most important thing, she reminded herself, was to "move those dogs" — all the dogs and not just Joey. But as she watched Snowy drive away in the Spencers' Range Rover in the seat where Joey should have sat, she felt crushed. After Mick's death, she had promised herself she would never get so attached to a shelter dog again. But it was easier said than done. She felt so bad now she didn't even want to look at Joey and see the trusting look in his eyes.

Nevertheless, she decided to stay at the shelter for the rest of the afternoon. She had no other plans, and figured she may as well help the other volunteer while she could.

It was after one o'clock when the Spencers left, and the midday sun suddenly turned scorching. It blazed down on the shelter courtyard turning its concrete sides and floor into a big kiln where the dogs were fired like clay. Even the rowdiest dogs were reduced to statues.

Her sadness over Joey meant Marjorie's heart wasn't in the job the way it should have been, and the heat made it worse. Yet if she was going to be of help, she knew she had better fix a smile on her lips, and wear it the whole day.

But the people she spoke to didn't make it easy. Some wandered through the shelter as if they were browsing for shoes. "No, sorry," they said as they breezed out the door. "Nothing here to suit us."

Others arrived with their children dressed for a day's

outing, as if they were at a fair, not a shelter. They took no notice of the terrified, sad or expectant looks on the dogs' faces; they were simply there to be entertained. Sometimes a mother would kneel down next to her young child, point at a dog, and say in toddler's English: "See the nice doggie. See, it wants to come out and play with you. Isn't that nice?" Meanwhile, the poor dog would bark eagerly in reply, hoping for a new home.

There were, however, people sincerely interested in finding a dog, and they were grateful to have Marjorie help them choose the right one. She, of course, would usher them to Joey's cage the moment they arrived, but while they liked his looks and felt sorry for him, they were always after something smaller or younger or fluffier or better trained.

Joey perked up every time anyone came near. He would get up despite the heat, raise his head, plant his feet firmly on the floor, and bark loudly at them. "Take me," he'd yell. "Please take me." His barking scared some people, but others heard the pleading in it. Then when the people moved on — and they always did — he would collapse to the ground again, unmoving but awake.

The afternoon dragged on this way 'til it was almost time for the shelter to close. Even so, it hadn't been a bad day. Besides Snowy, three other dogs had been adopted, leaving eighteen in the shelter. That was eighteen too many, Marjorie said to her volunteer partner, but it wasn't bad. She'd known days when there had been thirty-five. As long as no more were brought in, it meant no dogs would have to be put down for overcrowding. That, at least, was good news for Joey, and it was a thought Marjorie would cling to on her way home.

She was getting ready to leave when a woman dressed in a "Save the Rain Forest" T-shirt, faded jeans and sandals arrived with her daughter, a pretty girl with a raincloud of black hair falling loosely over a Minnie Mouse T-shirt.

"Hello," the woman greeted Marjorie, "My name is Barbara, and I'm looking for a dog for myself and my daughter, Melanie."

"Hello," Marjorie responded, not quite as eagerly as usual. It was the end of the day, and she was tired.

"Melanie's only five," Barbara continued, "and she hasn't had a dog before, but I think it would be good for her. My sister and I had a dog when we were girls, and I want Melanie to enjoy what we did. Can you help?"

"Of course I can," replied Marjorie, her enthusiasm starting to return. "That's why I'm here. What do you think, Melanie? Would you like a dog?"

"I think so," Melanie said, turning from side to side, a little shy of Marjorie. "I don't know."

"Well, we sure have some nice ones if you do."

Barbara told Marjorie that she was an accountant who worked out of her own house, so there was no danger of her having to move to a place where dogs wouldn't be allowed.

"That's good news," Marjorie said. "We always worry about landlords changing their minds and forcing animals out. Now, were you looking for a large dog or a small one?" She crossed her fingers that Barbara would say large.

She did. "Oh, a biggish dog, I think. A lab or a shepherd or a retriever, something like that. Maybe a mixture of all three. I don't know. But I'm sure I'll know when I see him. Or her."

"And that's all right with Melanie?" Marjorie asked. "She won't be afraid of a big dog?"

"Melanie, are you going to be afraid if we get a big dog?" Barbara asked her daughter. Melanie shook her head.

"A big dog it is then," Barbara said. "Show us the way."

Of course, Marjorie showed her the way to Joey, and as soon as Barbara set eyes on him, she wanted to adopt him. She didn't even want to walk him first.

Marjorie was struck dumb, which for Marjorie was as rare as an eclipse. But she was able to collect herself long enough to insist that Barbara take Joey for a walk so she could see how unmanageable he was. She hated doing that, but honesty was the best policy. "You don't have to," she said, "but it is a good idea. And the shelter will only let you if there's a volunteer to help. So you may as well. It is the best way of seeing what he's like. Often dogs act very differently once they're outside their cages."

"Fine," Barbara said. "If you really think it's necessary. We'll be careful."

Joey, however, wasn't. He sensed by the way Marjorie, Barbara and Melanie were acting, that something was up. The sight of the leash in Marjorie's hand made him sure of it. So he was on his feet, barking to be let out the moment they approached his cage. Even the heat didn't singe his enthusiasm, not when there was a walk to be had.

Marjorie thought it was all over as she watched Joey, who couldn't get over his good fortune, drag Barbara around the park like a tin can tied to a car. All those lessons on the leash had vanished in his excitement. "You see," he barked at Barbara as they circled the track, "you see how much fun we would have if you took me home? We could run this way all the time."

The thought of that made Joey want to run even faster. Imagine going for walks whenever I want, he thought. He got so worked up that he was ready to turn a somersault the way he had once seen some children do. But all he could manage was a sudden, vigorous leap. Marjorie hid her eyes when she saw that.

But Barbara wasn't bothered. "Yes, he is completely untrained," she said to Marjorie when she got back. "But I expected that. You don't come to an animal shelter expecting perfection, do you?"

"You'd be surprised how many people do," Marjorie replied.

"Well, I'm not one of those people," Barbara reassured Marjorie. "I want to adopt a dog who really needs a home, and since Joey has been in the shelter longer than any other dog, I want to adopt him. He's certainly young enough to be trained so I'll take him to obedience school, or get a book from the library, or find a friend who knows about dogs. It's not exactly rocket science, is it? But then I don't have to tell you that."

"No," laughed Marjorie. "You don't. But what about you, Melanie?" she said, kneeling down so she could look directly at the girl. "What do you think? Do you want to take Joey home with you?"

Melanie had stayed with Marjorie while Barbara and Joey had put each other through their paces, and sometimes she hadn't looked too happy about her mother's plan. When Joey had come out of his cage, she had put her hand out gingerly to pet him, but he had been so excited to be free that he tried to jump at her. If Marjorie hadn't been holding his leash, he might have knocked Melanie over.

Melanie shrugged her shoulders at the question, mumbled something Marjorie couldn't hear, and wrapped one arm around her mother's leg.

"Melanie, aren't you going to answer Marjorie?" Barbara asked.

Apparently not.

"Never mind," Barbara said, "Melanie will be fine. It's just a matter of her getting used to him. She'll probably be in love with him by tomorrow."

"It's just that I don't want to see him returned. Because if he were, the shelter staff might think he's unfit to be with a family and destroy him." She decided she had better be completely honest about this.

"Don't worry. I'm not going to return him. He's the dog for us. I know he's going to be a handful, but we'll get along. Don't worry," she repeated.

But Marjorie was worried. She couldn't believe that after all the effort she'd made finding Joey a home, she would have so many doubts, but she had. It wasn't that she didn't like Barbara; if Barbara had been on her own, she would have handed Joey over to her like a birthday present. It was Melanie who bothered her. What if she was afraid of Joey? What if she didn't grow to like him? What if he hurt her? The questions went round and round Marjorie's head like a ferris wheel.

As Barbara signed the adoption papers, Marjorie held tight to Joey's leash, worried that he might try to lunge at Melanie again. He didn't, but Melanie wasn't making any attempt to get to know him either. She just clung to her mother.

After Barbara paid the adoption fee, she led Joey out to her car with the handsome red collar and leash she'd bought from the shelter store. This time he couldn't have behaved better, and he hopped into the back seat as if he owned it. Melanie walked quietly beside them.

"Good-bye, Marjorie, and thanks so much for your

help," Barbara said, getting into her car. "And I have your phone number right here (she tapped the hip pocket of her jeans) so I'll be sure to phone you if there's a problem. But don't worry, there won't be."

Marjorie waved with one hand as she watched them drive off. The other she kept behind her back, its fingers crossed tightly. She hoped Barbara was right, but she had a bad feeling she hadn't seen the last of her.

Joey looked back at Marjorie briefly, but the sadness he felt at leaving her disappeared with the first rumble of Barbara's car engine. "This is it, Mick," he said silently. "This is really it. You and I are going home. No more shelter. No more cage. No more wandering the streets for garbage. This time we're going to a real home with a real family."

Barbara opened the car window so that a fresh breeze blew on Joey's face when the car started to move. It felt so good after the stale, sickly smell of the shelter. And instead of hard concrete under him, there was now a soft car seat. He squeezed himself into it as deeply as he could and faced straight ahead. His tongue hung lazily out of his mouth like an old sock, and his eyes shone bright as pennies.

seven

It didn't take long for Marjorie to hear from Barbara. Marjorie had planned to call her herself one day to find out how things were going, but five days after they had parted at the shelter, Barbara beat her to the dial.

"Hello, Marjorie," Barbara sang into the receiver. "This is Barbara, Joey's new mum."

Marjorie was caught off guard. She had seen too many so-called "confident" dog owners drive away with their new pets only to return them a week later because the dog had barked too loudly at a mail carrier or knocked over a favourite piece of crockery. Now she expected to hear something similar about Joey. "Yes, Barbara, of course," she said as cheerily as she could. "I was planning to call you myself, but I didn't want to call too soon. How's everything going?"

"Fine," Barbara said. "That's why I'm phoning, to say that everything's fine. I thought you'd like to know."

Marjorie was overcome with relief. "Of course I would.

I'm so glad to hear it."

"He did have a bit of a bad start, though," said Barbara. "Right on the dining room rug, if you know what I mean."

"I'm afraid I do," said Marjorie. "But I told you when you adopted him that he wasn't house-trained."

"Yes, you did, and you don't have to worry about it," Barbara replied. "I made it clear to him when it happened that he was not to do it again, and I think something sank in. In fact, I'd say he's well on his way to being trained now."

"Well, I told you he was a clever dog," said Marjorie, who was enjoying the talk now. "I knew that with the right person he'd be a terrific companion in no time. And how's he getting along with Melanie?" She felt fairly safe asking this because she was sure that if anything had gone wrong, she would have heard about it by now.

"Fine," Barbara answered again. "Melanie's really taking to him, and he seems to be crazy about her."

This is what Marjorie really wanted to hear. She was certain that once Melanie had made friends with Joey, everything would be set.

"That's marvellous," Marjorie said. "I'm so happy to hear it and everything else, and I'll be sure to tell all the other volunteers how well he's doing."

"Yes, please do. Because I'm pretty sure we're going to keep him. My sister thinks I'm crazy, but it's what Melanie and I think that counts, and we like him."

Barbara mentioning her sister that way was something

Marjorie would rather not have heard, but as the subject had been brought up, she felt she had to say something. "Oh, is there a problem with your sister?" she asked.

"Not really," Barbara said. "She came over to see Joey the day after we got him and she thought I was crazy to have such a large dog in the house. She also said if Melanie were her daughter, she wouldn't let Joey near her. But that's just my sister. As far as I'm concerned, everything's great. So don't worry."

Being told not to worry just made Marjorie worry even more, but what could she do? The whole thing was out of her hands.

In fact, Barbara's sister, Lucy, had caused more of a row than Barbara let on. She had acted as though she had seen a dragon, not a dog. After taking one stunned look at Joey, who was sitting on the living room rug next to Melanie with his mouth open and his teeth showing, she had yelled wildly and tried to rush her niece into the kitchen. But Melanie wouldn't go.

"Are you mad?" Lucy shouted at Barbara. "Why ever did you adopt a dog like that?"

"A dog like what?" replied Barbara who, though annoyed, was used to Lucy's outbursts.

"A dog like that!" Lucy shrieked. "A dog that size. A police dog. A dog that could tear Melanie to pieces."

"Oh, don't be so silly," said Barbara, stooping over to pet Joey, who had been a little alarmed by all the noise and movement. "He's not going to do anything to

Melanie. He's just a puppy — our puppy. Don't you remember the dog we had when we were kids? Well, I want Melanie to have a dog too."

But Lucy wouldn't calm down. She had just read in the newspaper about a dog attacking a little girl about Melanie's age, and she was sure the dog had been one like Joey.

"I tell you, Barbara, he's dangerous," she said. "What about that girl in the paper who was mauled?"

"Oh, for pity's sake," said Barbara, reaching down to rub Joey's chest. He had calmed down by then and begun to wag his tail. "Would you stop scaring Melanie with stories like that? This dog is not dangerous and he's not going to hurt anyone. Look at him." As she said this, almost as if he knew what was expected of him, Joey slathered Barbara's face with a sloppy kiss. The gesture wasn't lost on Lucy.

"Well ..." she began. "Maybe I am jumping to conclusions ... and I certainly didn't mean to frighten you," she turned to Melanie, who was only half-listening to the grown-ups. Then turning back to Barbara, "But I know what I read, and I tell you if it had been me, I would have got a chihuahua. You never know with dogs that big," she said, nodding at Joey. "They're unpredictable. Maybe you know what you're doing, but if I were you, I wouldn't take the chance."

After that, things settled down enough for Barbara to serve tea. Melanie went back to the game she was playing, and Barbara put Joey outside in the garden to make Lucy feel better. She really did believe Lucy was over-reacting, but she had been so upset that Barbara couldn't help wondering, if only for a second or two, if she'd been foolish to adopt Joey. Watching Joey run down the back steps, she wondered how much she really knew about him. No, she decided, shaking her head — Lucy had been ridiculous, and she wasn't going to give in to silly suspicions.

Joey would have preferred to stay inside with the family, but he liked the garden too. It was smaller than the LeClercs' garden, but it was more overgrown, with a lot of room for him to wander about and sniff. There was a fence to prevent him running away, but he wouldn't have done that even if he could. In the short time he'd been there, Joey had settled into Barbara's house as if he'd lived there all his life.

His new house was a place where a dog could really feel at home. It was full of warm, pleasant smells, soft surfaces and places where Joey could stretch out or curl up, depending on his mood. Unlike the LeClercs' house where everything was shiny, polished and off-limits, Barbara's house had a welcoming feel. There were fluffy cushions on the sofa and chairs, soft throw rugs on the carpet that looked to Joey as if they had been woven especially for him, and a fireplace that Barbara liked to use as often as she could when the weather cooled down.

Joey had settled into the house like an old pair of

slippers the first day. After the mess in the dining room had been cleaned up, and Joey had been scolded for it, he jumped up on Barbara's comfy sofa and curled up next to her. But she hadn't let him lie still for long. She had petted and pulled him and rolled him over to rub his tummy. It made him feel wonderful, and he knew that at long last he'd found the home he'd always wanted.

Barbara and Melanie also had taken him for a long walk. That hadn't been quite the treat he had hoped for since Barbara insisted on keeping him on a leash, and she pulled hard on it every time he tried to bolt, just the way the volunteers in the shelter had. But she hadn't been cruel about it. Walking on a leash was something he'd just have to get used to, he decided, no matter how much he didn't like it.

But Lucy had upset him. He couldn't understand why she had pulled Melanie away from him so suddenly, and he worried that something was terribly wrong. He'd been relieved when Barbara started stroking him, and felt she deserved a kiss.

After that, things went smoothly for several weeks. Melanie, as Barbara said she would, grew more and more attached to Joey, and Joey grew calmer around both of them. He was fully house-trained in just over a week, and was making some progress learning how to heel, sit and stay. Nevertheless, Barbara continued to worry about what Lucy had said. Once when a repairman came to the door, Joey barked so violently that the repairman refused to come inside. "Joey!" Barbara yelled. "Be quiet!" "Sorry," she said to the repairman who was backing away from the door. "He's just a bit over-protective, that's all. He won't hurt you, will you Joey?" she said, turning back to Joey. Then to the repairman again: "Please come inside. I really am sorry."

After that, everything was fine because Joey trusted Barbara and decided that if she said the man was okay, he must be okay. But the repairman had looked awfully like the man who'd come after Joey with a club, and Joey didn't want to take any chances.

The episode had upset Barbara, but still Joey showed no signs of being dangerous, and she took comfort in what Marjorie had said about him being brought up in a house with a child. But why had he barked so viciously at the repairman? That wasn't like him at all. She too had read about the little girl being mauled, and hard as she tried, she sometimes couldn't get the story out of her mind. What Lucy had failed to mention was that though the offending dog was a German shepherd, he had been trained as a guard dog and been mistreated all his life. He had attacked out of a kind of madness. Joey would never do that. On the other hand, Barbara wondered, hadn't he been mistreated in the shelter just by being there? Before Barbara had adopted Joey, friends of hers had advised her to buy a puppy from a breeder, but she pooh-poohed the idea saying it would be too expensive and she'd rather give a home to a dog who really needed one. But had she been wrong? Perhaps, she thought, it was time to phone Marjorie again.

She tried to hide the concern in her voice, but Marjorie was too sharp for that. She knew something was wrong. Why else would Barbara be phoning?

"Hello, Barbara. How are you? And how's my beautiful boy?" She hoped being cheerful would make it harder for Barbara to break any bad news.

"Fine, thank you, and he's lovely," Barbara enthused. "He's house-trained now, and he's learning to walk on the leash without pulling. I can even make him sit and come on command … sometimes," she laughed. "No, he really is fine. Couldn't be better."

"Well, that's wonderful. I'm so glad to hear it," said Marjorie, very surprised, and hopeful now that that was all Barbara had wanted to say.

"There is just one thing," Barbara said before Marjorie could hang up. "Is there something I should know about Joey that you didn't tell me at the shelter?"

Ah hah, thought Marjorie, this is why she phoned. "Such as what?" she replied, wondering what lay behind the question. She honestly couldn't think of a thing.

"Well, you said he was brought up in a house where there was a little boy. Did he ever try to hurt the boy?" Barbara asked.

"No, of course not," Marjorie blurted out. She certainly hadn't expected that. "Why ever do you ask? Has he tried to hurt Melanie?" She was frightened now since it had been Melanie whom she'd been worried about all along.

"No, no," Barbara said. "He's been fine with her. Perfect. No, it's just that ... I know it's silly, but given how my sister was about Joey ... and then there was that story in the paper about the German shepherd who attacked the little girl. Did you see it? You even said yourself that you were worried about how he'd be with Melanie when we brought him home. It's all got me wondering if after having been in the shelter for so long that Joey might be ... how shall I put it ...?"

"Dangerous?" suggested Marjorie. She couldn't believe what she was hearing. But what could she say? There was no question that Barbara's daughter came first, and if Barbara had doubts about Joey, no matter how Marjorie felt about him, he would have to be returned. But she hoped it wouldn't go that far.

"Really, Barbara," she said, "if you're at all worried about Melanie's safety ..." She hated to come right out and say it. "I promise you that there's no reason to be, but if you are ..."

"No, I'm not," said Barbara. Talking to Marjorie this way began to make her feel foolish, and she decided not to tell her about the repairman. "I just wanted to talk to you so that you could put my mind at rest. And you have. After all, there are thousands of German shepherds out there, and how many of them hurt children? One, and then the papers make a big deal out of it. No, it's just my silly sister and then that silly newspaper report. I just wanted to be sure, that's all."

"I don't know what to say," said Marjorie. "I promise you the people who brought Joey to the shelter said nothing about him being dangerous. I was there and heard everything they said. And while he was in the shelter, he was as good as gold. A bit too lively at times, but he never tried to hurt anyone. All he did was bark a lot."

"Did he?" Barbara was surprised. That would explain his reaction to the repairman. "Well, he still does, but only when he's excited. No, really, Marjorie. There's nothing to worry about. I'm just being stupid. I'm going to put the whole thing out of my mind."

"If you're sure," said Marjorie. She hoped for everyone's sake that Barbara was.

"Yes, I'm positive," Barbara said. "I'm sorry to have bothered you. Please forget the whole thing."

But even then she wasn't sure. No matter how good Joey was — and he couldn't have been better — she continued to be rattled by doubts. Women Joey didn't know never bothered him, but he always seemed nervous around strange men. Whenever one came to the door, he would bark until Barbara told him to stop. Memories of being out on the street still haunted Joey, and men's voices reminded him of the men who'd been cruel to him. When Barbara told him to be quiet, he always was, and when he got to know the man, he usually liked him. Barbara appreciated that, but she wondered why he had to bark in the first place.

The friends who had suggested she buy a puppy agreed now that Joey was lovely, but they remained convinced that because he had lived with another family before Barbara's, he might not be as loyal to Barbara and Melanie as he would be if he'd been theirs from the start. He would never really belong, they said, no matter how good he is. "They're right," Lucy said. "Yes, Joey is a nice dog," (she had long since got over being afraid of him), "but I still don't understand why you had to get a dog from the shelter. Especially a dog that size."

Joey didn't know about any of this. As far as he was concerned, everything was perfect. He loved Barbara. He loved Barbara's house and garden. And he loved Melanie. He also loved the long walks Barbara and Melanie took him on, especially when they let him off the leash to play with other dogs in the park. He devoured the treats they fed him and the raw eggs they put in his food to make his coat gleam. And when they watched TV, he always lay down beside them.

Whenever Melanie had her friends Carol and Jennifer over, they would go to her bedroom to play, and Melanie always insisted that Joey join them. "Joey's my friend too," she would say to her mother and guests. Then she'd run over to Barbara and whisper, "Joey's really my best friend, but I can't tell Carol and Jennifer that."

Sometimes these parties included what came to be known as "Joey's singing." Melanie had been given a harmonica by her uncle, and when she played it, Joey would "sing" along. He did it when Melanie's friends played too. He would lift his chin in the air, gaze at his audience to make sure they were listening, and then bay at the ceiling as if there were someone up there listening as well. Later, Barbara got him his own footstool. Then as soon as Melanie got out the harmonica, he would rest his front paws on the stool like a seal on a rock, and begin his concert. Melanie and her friends couldn't get enough of it. They would clap and cheer and fall over each other laughing. Then when he finished, Joey would beam at them with delight.

Yet Barbara had been unhappy with the game at first. She worried about leaving Joey alone in a room with such young children. She phoned the other girls' mothers to tell them about it, but none of them cared. Fine, they all said, their daughters loved animals.

"Okay," Barbara said, "as long as you know."

Then something happened to change things. As usual, Barbara and Melanie decided to take Joey for a walk to the park. They always went to the same park, and Joey knew the routine well. As soon as they got there, they would let him off his leash and he would run around in every direction, especially when there were other dogs to chase and play with. But he always kept an eye on his family and came whenever they called. What was different this time was that a strange man — dressed in a long overcoat, heavy shoes and a hat — was in the park, and the man was walking toward them. Even though it was mid-autumn by then, it was still warm, so Barbara thought the man was dressed a little oddly, but she reminded herself: "Live and let live," and tried not to think about it any more.

But instead of walking around them, the man carried on straight toward them. Melanie was nervous as soon as she saw him, but Barbara told her not to worry. "He's just out for a walk," she whispered. "There's nothing to be afraid of."

The man didn't say anything, but Joey, sensing Melanie's fear, began barking at the man and baring his teeth at him. Barbara told Joey to stop and calm down, but he refused.

"Joey, stop that!" Barbara yelled. "Leave the man alone!" But Joey carried on. This was one time, he decided, when disobeying Barbara was the right thing to do.

The man, who was quite close by then, began backing away, but he kept his eyes fixed on them.

"I'm sorry," Barbara reassured him. "It's just the way Joey is with strangers. You mustn't be frightened. He'll calm down. Won't you, Joey?" she said as sternly as she could, glaring at Joey.

The man didn't reply, and Joey continued to bark.

"Joey!" Barbara shouted. "What is wrong with you?

Be quiet right now!"

But still Joey wouldn't. Barbara tried to hold onto his collar, but he pulled so hard on it that she had to let go.

As she did, Joey barked, "Get out of here!" at the man, who had started to run away. "Get out of here!" he roared, and gave chase.

"Joey!" Barbara screamed after him. "Come back here at once! I mean it! At once!"

But Joey chased the man to the other side of the park where all of a sudden the man spun around and shook a knife in Joey's face. "Get out of here, you bloody dog, or you're gonna get this!" he shouted, waving the knife. He was too far away for Barbara to see or hear him. All she could see was Joey still barking and misbehaving.

"Joey! Joey! Joey!" she kept yelling, starting to run after him herself. "Come back here now!"

The man was still waving the knife, but Joey had chased him far enough not to be a danger to Barbara or Melanie any more. So it was safe to go back to them.

"Joey!" Barbara yelled at the top of her lungs when they met. "Are you crazy? What on earth are you doing?!" She put his leash back on his collar and led him, swiftly and angrily, out of the park and back home. Melanie ran after them.

Barbara had calmed down somewhat by the time they got home, but she was still upset. Yes, she had to admit that the man had looked a little sinister, but that wasn't the point. Joey's behaviour was. He'd gone berserk. Lucy was right, she would be better off with a smaller dog or no dog at all. Joey simply couldn't be trusted around strangers any more. What would he do next time? Go for someone's throat? No, she couldn't risk it. Joey would have to go. So much as she hated to do it, she phoned Marjorie, explained what had happened, and insisted that the shelter take him back.

Marjorie was heartbroken and bewildered. She would have understood if Joey had attacked the man, but it seemed to her that all he'd done was try to protect Melanie. Barbara should have been proud of him for that, she thought, not angry. She tried to make Barbara see that, but Barbara wouldn't be moved.

"I'm sorry, Marjorie. I truly am. But I was there, you weren't. I saw Joey chase the man, I heard him growl and I saw him bare his teeth. And I'm not going to allow that to happen again. It's too dangerous. No matter what you say, I think I'd better bring him back."

Marjorie still thought she was wrong, but she had to give in. She had no choice. Not that she liked it one bit. If Joey really were dangerous, he wouldn't have a chance at the shelter. They'd have to put him down. "Will you be returning him tomorrow?" Marjorie asked through clenched teeth. She was afraid that if she wasn't careful, she would say something she might regret.

"No," Barbara said, "I have to think about how I'm going to explain it to Melanie, and I promised to take her on an outing tomorrow. I don't want to spoil that.

The day after will be soon enough. I'm sure he won't do any harm between now and then."

"No, Barbara, I'm sure he won't," Marjorie said, trying to make a point.

Barbara ignored it. "Will you be at the shelter to see him when he comes in?" she asked.

Marjorie saw no reason why she should be — she certainly didn't want to do Barbara any favours — but then decided she better be there to speak up for Joey to the shelter staff. She didn't want him to be put down unfairly as a dangerous dog. "Yes, I'll be there," she said as coldly as she could. "At one o'clock. I'll be looking for you."

"Okay, one o'clock. I'll be there. And Marjorie, I really am sorry."

"Yes, well, I'm sorry too," Marjorie said. Then she hung up.

Barbara had promised to help Melanie gather fallen leaves the next day so they could press them into pictures in a scrapbook. She said they'd have a picnic too if it were warm enough. They were going to a place north of the city that was more like a piece of wilderness than a park. A fast-flowing river cut through the park, and though it was too dangerous to swim in, it was lovely to look at and sit beside. They had been there several times, so Melanie knew the exact spot where she wanted to lay their blanket.

She also wanted Joey to come with them. She wanted

him to go everywhere with them. "That's what dogs are for," she said. So she couldn't understand when, that evening before going to bed, her mother told her they were going to leave him at home.

"No, Mummy," she cried. "He has to come. He's our dog."

"I know he is, Darling," Barbara said. "But this time it might be better to leave him at home. Remember what happened in the park today?"

Melanie screwed up her face and thought. Yes, she remembered the strange-looking man, and how Joey had barked and run after him.

"Yes," Melanie said, "I remember."

"Well, I don't want that to happen again. I don't want Joey barking at anyone else the same way. Do you understand?"

"No," Melanie argued, "I don't. I still want Joey to come. Please let him come on the picnic with us, Mummy. Pleeeease. I don't want to go at all if he can't."

In the end, she made such a fuss that Barbara had to give in. She knew how upset Melanie would be when they returned Joey to the shelter, so she decided she may as well let her be happy while she could.

"But we'll have to be careful with Joey," she warned. "We don't want him barking at any more strangers."

"Okay," said Melanie, and then forgot all about it.

The next day rose Indian summer hot and beautiful, and Melanie couldn't wait to get to the park and her favourite place by the river. Neither could Joey. He knew car rides usually meant going somewhere fun. So when he saw Barbara taking things out to the driveway, he wagged his tail like a fan, and rushed out to join her, barking with anticipation.

"Shut up, Joey!" she barked back at him. "I'm sick and tired of all your noise."

Joey was as surprised as if she'd kicked him. The only time Barbara ever shouted at him was when he did something wrong. But what had he done this time? He stopped barking and jumped into the back seat of the car.

"Joey!" Barbara yelled again. "Come out of there! And don't move until I tell you to."

Joey jumped out and froze in his tracks, more puzzled than ever. The back seat was where he always sat with Melanie. But not this time. When they finally got going, Melanie sat in the front seat with her mother. Joey didn't mind much since he now had the whole back seat to stretch out on, but he still thought it was strange.

It was the same in the park. Joey was delighted to be in such a wild place with such interesting sounds and smells, but Barbara wouldn't let him enjoy them properly.

"Joey, come here!" she shouted if he strayed only a few feet ahead of her. And whenever another person walked by, she would yell even louder at him and grab his collar so hard she almost throttled him.

He always obeyed because he loved Barbara, but he couldn't understand why she was so jumpy. It wasn't like her at all.

Things settled down a bit while they ate their picnic. Barbara and Melanie had sandwiches and lemonade, while Joey enjoyed his dog biscuits and water. He knew not to beg for food, but to wait until it was offered. Usually it was, but not today. Today Barbara was in no mood to spoil him, and when Melanie offered him a piece of her sandwich, Barbara made her take it back.

"Joey's fine as he is," she told Melanie.

"But Mum … " Melanie began.

"Melanie," Barbara said firmly, "That's enough."

When they finished eating, Melanie wanted to walk along the river and throw stones into it. The river was a lovely turquoise colour, frothy with white foam as it leaped and danced past them like a parade on its way to the sea. Every now and then, it would relax into small pools that looked as if they might be good for swimming if it weren't for the fierce rapids that rushed in and out of them. To prevent people from jumping or falling in, a wire fence had been put up along the river's edge.

Melanie skipped happily along the path next to the fence. In one hand, she held a bouquet of leaves she had collected, all red and gold like the colours of a sunset. With the other, she picked up stones and tossed them through the fence into the water, enjoying the plop and splash they made when they broke the surface. Barbara followed a few steps behind with Joey close beside her. She held him so close that sometimes he would lose his footing and stumble over the rocks and roots in the path. But frustrated as he was, he never complained.

In fact, Barbara was so caught up in keeping an eye on Joey that she began to lose sight of Melanie. She didn't notice that farther along the path, the fence had been torn open, leaving a large, dangerous hole.

All Barbara heard was a scream and a splash. When she looked up to see what it was, she felt Joey's leash wrench out of her hand so violently that she thought her skin had come off with it. Then in a flash she caught sight of his tail as he jumped through the hole and into the river after Melanie.

The pool Melanie had fallen into was dangerously near a set of rapids. She thrashed and screamed and tried to swim away from them, but the more she thrashed, the more water she swallowed. As Joey raced toward her, he could see her head going under once, then twice.

When Joey finally reached Melanie, she grabbed on and held tight to his neck for dear life. Joey thought his heart would burst as he turned and tried to fight his way back to shore against the river's fierce flow. But he wouldn't give up. Not for anything.

Sometimes Melanie's struggling forced Joey's head under water so he couldn't see anything except white water churning around him. But he kept swimming. Barbara was on shore hollering and waving, and with

each push and pull he could see that they were getting nearer to her. It wasn't a long way to the river bank, but having to swim against the current made it seem twice as far.

Other hikers had heard screams and were now gathered anxiously at the shore. One man slipped down into the water to reach for Joey and Melanie as they drew nearer, while other people held onto him to make sure he wasn't swept away too. The crowd let out a cheer when he finally grabbed them and pulled them to safety.

"Melanie," Barbara whispered through her tears. "Oh Melanie, Melanie."

"Mummy, Mummy," Melanie cried between shivers. "I was so scared, Mummy." But she was too cold and upset to say any more.

"Oh, Melanie," Barbara said again. "My darling little girl. Thank God I have you back."

Then Barbara remembered Joey. She turned to find him smiling at her in that way he had, his tongue drooping out of his mouth like a flat, pink fish as he panted the breath back into his lungs. Like Barbara, all that mattered to him was that Melanie was safe, and the family he loved more than anything in the world was still together.

"Joey!" Barbara cried, rushing over to him and wrapping her arms around his neck. "My wonderful, wonderful boy."

Then she began to cry even harder. Melanie hugged

Joey and cried too. Joey pressed himself close to both of them, and none of them wanted to ever let go.

After that, there was no question of returning Joey to the animal shelter. He was a hero. He even had his picture taken for the morning newspaper, and there it was smack on the front page the next day. Under a caption reading: "Every dog has his day," the story read:

> *Five-year-old Melanie Cooper was rescued from drowning by her dog, Joey, yesterday, after she fell into Winston River. Witnesses said Joey jumped in after the girl and pulled her safely to shore. Melanie's mother, Barbara Cooper, had adopted Joey from the animal shelter, and said it was the best thing she had ever done. Melanie was taken to hospital for observation, but hospital officials said she was in good condition and would be released today.*

Marjorie saw the picture as she was sitting down to breakfast. She was so thrilled that she knocked over a milk jug and almost spit out her corn flakes. Whooping with joy, she spun around the room, and thrust the newspaper into her husband's face. "See," she said, "that's why I do what I do."

But pleased as she was, she wasn't all that surprised.

She knew Joey had it in him. She knew what all the shelter dogs could be if only they were given a chance. Most important, she knew Barbara wouldn't be keeping their appointment that afternoon. Nonetheless she decided to go to the shelter to wave Joey's picture under Mr. Forrester's nose and pin it to the office bulletin board. Today of all days, she wanted to do what she could to help move more dogs. At last count, there were twenty-two waiting and hoping for homes, and that was twenty-two too many.

Mr. and Mrs. LeClerc saw the story too, but they didn't want to say anything about it to Robert. He was feeling bad enough after twisting his ankle falling off his new mountain bike. But he saw it anyway.

"I told you we should have kept him!" he yelled at his parents. "I told you we should have kept him! I told you all along!"

Joey loved the attention being heaped on him, but he couldn't really understand what it was all about. Melanie had fallen in the water and he had jumped in after her. What else was he supposed to have done? But people kept saying how amazing it was for such a young dog to have done such a brave deed. Even Lucy had given him a big hug when she saw him, and then had burst into tears herself.

Come to think of it, Joey thought, there had been a lot of crying going on ever since they got back from the park. But he was happy. He had a home where the people wanted him, and if those people wanted to wail and cry and carry on, that was okay too. It was just as Marguerite, the cat, had said: Humans were strange creatures who did strange things.

So Joey just kept smiling when people stopped to pet him and tell him what a splendid dog he was. He wasn't about to turn down that kind of praise. But if anyone had bothered to ask, what he really would have liked was a good long run.

About the Author

Nicholas Read is a columnist and radio broadcaster who specializes in animal issues. He has been awarded the Canadian Federation of Humane Societies Journalism Award, the Royal Society for the Protection of Animals Journalism Award (UK) and the International Society for Animal Rights Media Award (USA). He lives in England and works for Animal Aid, an animal rights organization.